perfectly

Crazy

Mitzi Penzes

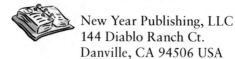 New Year Publishing, LLC
144 Diablo Ranch Ct.
Danville, CA 94506 USA

Sept. 2F. 2011.

To Lisa with hugs and appreciation!

To my son Ali, who made me realize how
limitless love is

...and to Nelly and Pista for giving me inspiration
for this book, the best parents to have.

Mitu.

1

Nell was a looker, and she knew it, too. Everywhere she went, men noticed her. This would have been excellent if she had wanted a man, but she did not. She did not want *a* man, she wanted a particular one. She deserved and wanted the *perfect* man.

Now, the word might mean different things for different women, but for her there was only one "perfect." The problem was that David was married to another woman, although Nell's marriage and two children did not her make attraction any easier to bear. She'd been married to Jack for sixteen years now, and from the outside her marriage seemed pretty solid and happy. And it was! People thought that you couldn't be happy without finding your perfect mate, but it wasn't true. Still, she'd always wondered what being with David would be like.

As for David, he was happy with Julie, too. At least, there was the appearance of a good and balanced relationship. But it had to be a little hollow; if it weren't, then David would not have come to Nell so often to complain and ask for marital advice.

Now, in recent months, this had given Nell some encouragement to fantasize about their future together. It might be perfectly crazy and definitely unexpected, but somehow she had a feeling that an impending change would be coming in their relationship. Perhaps they would not stay best friends, and their closeness would change to intimacy. She felt expectant, excited, and a little confused, not to mention guilty.

There was a yearning in her that hadn't been there before, and although it was unexplained, its existence was undeniable.

Today, she and David had met for drinks in his penthouse apartment. They'd sat down together on the couch, and she was looking at him now. What a gorgeous man! Dark hair, straight nose, chiseled features, and expressive eyes. They were ocean blue, and they could melt any woman into a puddle on command. Nell was feeling the effect already. Lately, she was conscious of feeling palpitations and excitement every time she was near David. And near she was, indeed, since he was scooting closer every minute on the settee. By now, their thighs were touching. David put his arm casually over her shoulder, and even though it seemed like an easy and natural move, for Nell it was anything but. The place where his fingers touched her arm through the blouse felt very hot. His breath had a little mint on it, and the fact that she was close enough to smell it made her almost dizzy. "So, what should I do now? Does she really expect me to come home and perform on schedule?" he said. "I don't see how continuing the Nelson lineage is that important! If it's in our future, okay. But working for it like nothing else matters...it's just not right. Julie's normally so soft and easily swayed. Not this time!"

"Okay, David, I understand you feel pressured, but you have to consider the differences between men and women," replied Nell. "She has her biological clock ticking. As for you, if you live long like your ancestors, you might have another sixty years to have a kid. You know I don't usually take Julie's side, but this time she might just have a reason to rush you, babe."

David pulled her even closer, so now she could smell his hair and his aftershave. He had a smell Nell could kill for, and she was sure thousands of women would do the same if they got to be so close. Ah, the sacrifices of friendship...

"She's only thirty-four! And as for me making babies at age one hundred, your theory might have some flaws, sweetheart. By the way, I love when you call me 'babe.' It makes me feel even younger."

"Younger than what? Incidentally, I like it when you call me 'sweetheart' as well. As for my theory, now that you really make me think about it, I'm getting a visual of you procreating as an old man. And—oh, no! It's not a pretty picture."

By this time, David's nearness had left Nell in a state of complete excitement. It took her a great deal of effort to look unaffected, and she hoped like hell he hadn't noticed her ever-growing excitement. Even though she clearly desired to claim him as her own, she was torn. Which was the stronger pull? Sixteen years of solid marriage, or *complete* happiness with the man of her dreams?

David's laugh brought her back from her daydreaming, and she was both pleased and surprised by his next statement. "You know, my pet, if it was *you* waiting for me, I wouldn't ever mind coming home to do my duty."

"What?" Nell hoped she sounded normal, and not as agitated as she felt inside.

"I was just telling you, coming home to you probably wouldn't be stressful at all. But it certainly is with Julie! She just looks at me and expects me to jump into it, do my sex act, and leave. Not that I miss the conversation afterward, but she doesn't have the slightest clue about how to make a man hot or excited. No fantasy, no role playing, no sexy lingerie, nothing. She might as well be asking for a sandwich. It doesn't work for me. Don't get me wrong, it doesn't prevent me having sex with her, but somehow, I don't look forward to it anymore."

"And how would it be different with me, pray?" asked Nell with a slight smile.

"You just walk anywhere, and with your smile, your demeanor, your posture…You make a man think of sex and nothing else. I bet you're resourceful when it comes to making your man excited. Hell, just looking at me like that, you make me hot."

With that, he grabbed the back of her neck with one hand and lowered his mouth to hers for a kiss.

This was not only a surprise, but completely uncharted territory. They'd always teased each other, joked, and he'd usually grab, pet, or otherwise touched her when they were on their own, but he'd never done this before. It was a good thing he hadn't kissed her before, because if he'd done it, Nell would have never been able to wait years to have the same experience again. No way. This was out of this world!

Instead of pulling back, she opened her mouth to him and pulled him closer...until reality finally set in. Then she pulled back quickly. They looked at each other, spooked and out of breath.

"Please, David! You know we can't do this!" Her voice was so weak it sounded pathetic.

For almost a minute it was quiet except for their hard breathing.

For David, it felt like the hardest thing in his life not to grab her again and continue with what they'd started. He knew they were wrong to do it, but it still felt so right. What surprised him the most was the fact that he'd never realized how much he wanted Nell. The truly scary part was that he was sure his feelings were far too strong to be merely a passing desire. He did not want to just stop here, forget that it had ever happened, and go back home to his dutiful wife. He'd never before experienced this kind of unbearably strong need. In that instant, he realized clearly how his feelings toward his own wife had weakened, shifted, lost their urgency.

"You know, this was bound to happen, since we're so attuned to each other and have been friends for so long. But you know as well as me that we can't ruin our friendship this way!" said Nell. But even she didn't seem convinced. She was pushing herself up from the settee and trying to straighten her clothes. Her chest was still rising and falling rapidly, and her face was flushed. *She's the loveliest, sexiest woman*, David thought to himself.

"Look, we can't disappoint our families this way to gratify ourselves. So let's just go back to where we started. Let's cool off, give ourselves a little time, and avoid each other for a few days, shall we?" said Nell.

With that, she marched to the door and was about to leave, but David reached her in two strides and grabbed her from behind. "I know you're trying to be fair, and I know I should agree, but if you think this is the end, you're gravely mistaken. From this moment on, I'll never be able to see you again without thinking about this kiss and where it could lead. We could pretend it was just a fluke, but I know it's not, and you know it, too. Although honor and decency tell me not to pursue you again…I don't think I can just let it go, sweetheart. Life is too short."

He let her arm go so fast, Nell almost fell over. Then in a few strides he was out of his apartment, where they'd spent so many hours together before. It was a penthouse in a high rise in downtown San Diego, with the loveliest view of the harbor. She'd often just sat at the huge glass wall, looking at the cruise ships and all the busy activities that went on below in the harbor.

Now she was looking at the empty doorframe. For minutes, she could not even move. *I have to just go on and live my life as I did until now. But it's going to be very, very hard!* she thought.

At that very moment, her phone rang. She examined her beloved iPhone, and, seeing it was her daughter, Chelsea, she answered. "Yes, love, what is it?"

"Mom, I'm done with swim practice. If I go over to Michelle's place for an hour or so, would you mind picking me up later?"

"Okay."

"Mom, are you okay? You sound a little strange," said Chelsea.

"I'm fine, darling, just a little tired. I'll pick you up around six, then."

She disconnected and sat down on the settee to think things over. *I might be here a while!* she said to herself. *I have a lot to mull over, for sure. But I can take the time. Chelsea will be fine with her friend's family.*

Her thoughts turned to her husband, Jack, and his last phone call. He was a busy plastic surgeon, and he was always working. So she'd been surprised when he'd suggested in the call that they should go on a weekend vacation somewhere, on their own, to relax. He'd said he missed being with her and enjoying her just for himself. *Does he sense somehow I have feelings for another man? He hasn't said anything like that, but the last time he suggested a weekend just for us must have been five years ago.*

She thought their marriage was solid and fine. Even the sex was great. She always enjoyed sex, no matter what; no special skill on any man's part was needed to pull out her passion. She was just a blessed woman who loved sex. Not that Jack wasn't a considerate, skilled lover; in fact, he was even romantic on occasion, getting her roses, chocolates, and jewelry.

Lately, she'd sometimes wondered how it would feel to have David touching her, though. Would his lovemaking be different? Better? Would he be a better kisser?

Well, as for the kisses, now she knew. He'd made her dizzy in a few seconds. It had been the best damn kissing she'd ever had; out of a scale of 1 to 10, it must have been a 13!

She was now very confused. On the one hand, she had her long-standing, normal relationship with Jack. On the other hand was David, who seemed to be going through the same transition as her. He was taken with her, just as she was with him. *What should I do now? Is this something I must suppress, or can I somehow let myself pursue this feeling? It's so very powerful...*

but is it the right thing to do? She rubbed her forehead. *Somehow I'll solve this problem. It might take time, but I can do anything!*

She repeated this motto to herself, then picked up her designer bag, put on her three-inch heels, checked herself in the mirror, and left the apartment. It was time to salvage the rest of the day and take care of all the mundane things that needed to be done. *Tomorrow is always another day,* just like Scarlet O'Hara said, she thought, and stepped into the elevator.

As expected, downstairs in the lobby she got all the attention she needed. The nice doorman calling for her car; the guy delivering her shiny red Cobra—they were all smiles. Men just loved her, and she had to admit to herself, she still looked good. Her high cheekbones and almond-shaped, green eyes made her face a little catlike, an effect that was even more powerful when she smiled, showing even, white teeth. Her hair was red and, although colored, was very well styled and shiny. Her long earrings dangled enticingly, and her small skirt showed off her legs. According to Jack, they were as sexy and as well formed as Josephine Baker's. She had seen a photo of Baker, and she thought that was a very nice compliment, indeed.

Yeah, I still look good, she thought to herself, *but soon, time will take all this prettiness.* She was not a worrier; it was something to deal with later, not now.

2

"*So,* have you been thinking about my vacation idea?" asked Jack. They were at home, and he was peering at her above his reading glasses. He looked a little tired, but still very handsome. He was the best-looking surgeon at his hospital—even the best-looking man on the whole staff. He was fifty-eight, but he had excellent posture, was nicely muscled from working out, and had little silver streaks at his temples that made him look even more distinguished. Nell knew that many of his patients had the hots for him, not to mention the nurses, who gave him their best just for a smile. He had the warmest smile, and he really cared how his patients felt. Nell always loved that about him.

"So, do you have any good ideas about places? I was thinking about Hawaii. We haven't been there for ages," Jack continued.

"Look, I don't want to sound suspicious, but it's been ages since you suggested a trip just for the two of us. What's going on? Is everything okay?"

She must have looked worried, because Jack lifted up his palms almost defensively. "Can't a man just want to spend a little quality time with his wife?" he answered, smiling. Then his tone grew serious. "But, Nell...there is something I've been meaning to tell you. I've been feeling a little more tired than usual. And...I've had some weakness in my fingers lately. So I've sent out a lab request to see if my muscles are fine, or if there's something starting..."

"What?" Nell felt stunned.

"I meant to tell you on the vacation, but now you've started asking questions, I can't hide it from you. Nell, I'm checking to see if I have Parkinson's or some other neuromuscular disease—"

"Did you have any tremors or spasms as well?" Nell was an MD herself, and had been a pretty successful eye surgeon until she'd given up her practice to start a fashion retail business. So she knew what a devastating possibility Jack was talking about. His career would be down the tubes, and worse, neuromuscular diseases were usually devastating and chronic.

"Not yet," said Jack, "but I wonder about the future…"

"Calm down. You're probably just thinking of the worst possibilities," said Nell, forcing herself to calm down as well. "Even if you end up being ill, we can afford for you to retire. After all, you just turned fifty-eight."

"Can you imagine me sitting at home, wasting away instead of working? No way!"

"Let's not jump to conclusions," said Nell firmly. "Probably you're just a little overworked. Look, I think going away to Hawaii is a great idea. I can get tickets for next Monday. Do you want to spend a week?"

"Yeah, that'd be great!" But he didn't sound too convinced.

"Good. It's settled. And you know what else will take your mind off things? A fundraiser ball! It's going to be this weekend, remember? We'll go with David and Julie. I've already got the costumes ready. We'll be king and queen," said Nell.

Despite her positive tone, she felt completely out of sorts. First she had her kiss with David to worry about, and now Jack's possible illness. She hoped things would straighten out soon.

At that moment, her phone beeped. David had texted her. *I just found out I will see u at the fundraiser tomorrow. We need to talk. If not there, then soon. I will be a gondolier. J says you will be a queen. How fitting! I can't wait.*

She excused herself from Jack, and went in the kitchen so she could text back. *Talk has to wait. I will go for a short trip next week. Maybe after that?*

Where are u going? Jack texted back.

Not that it is any of your business, but Hawaii. Jack needs a break.

The heck it's not my business! Is Jack OK? Say hi to him for me.

I'll tell u about it later. Say hi to Julie for me, too.

With that, she headed for the shower so she could try to get her mind off all these new developments. She doubted she'd be able to. She decided she'd get into her favorite robe and try to read something. Or perhaps she'd convince Jack to watch a funny movie with her; he'd seemed so dejected, and she didn't want him to think about unpleasant stuff for a while. *Well, good luck with that...*she thought.

When she came back, Jack was already in bed, and as soon as she slipped under the quilt, he scooted over and kissed her neck.

"I thought you were tired," she said.

"Not *that* much! Even if I was, you're just too sexy, beautiful."

His touch felt wonderful and arousing. *He's a very sexy man himself,* Nell thought. She let the sensation engulf her and reciprocated in earnest, but there was a little part of her mind that felt unaffected. Somehow, even in the throes of her passion, she felt detached, and she'd never noticed this feeling before. Was it because of her feelings for David?

Afterward, she listened to Jack's soft snoring and thought some more. *Would it be different if I had David?* she wondered. But something had changed with that kiss. Now that he'd finally noticed they shared more than friendship, Nell felt different herself. For the first time in her life, she wondered if sex could be even better than what she'd just had.

I wonder if I'll ever experience something so powerful as that kiss again? she thought, and drifted off to sleep uneasily.

3

That Sunday evening, Nell and Jack arrived at the ball in a limo. They were surprised at the large turnout. The people filing in had the most outrageous and inventive costumes, so their king and queen outfits were almost too boring to be compared to some of them. There were spacemen and aliens, Renaissance princesses and monks, a few Elvises, some Grim Reapers, and wolves, swans, and cartoon characters. It was dazzling.

Nell hadn't really wanted to be the best costumed, but she'd thought most people wouldn't go all-out spending their money or time on dressing up. She was wrong. Most of the costumes were very elaborate, probably expensive, and there were a few that could be called pretty original as well. Still, Nell thought that she and Jack had done well themselves, all in all. Her embroidered, silk-and-velvet dress and crown were beautifully tailored. Jack was a dashing king, and the sword hanging at his side made him look like he was ready for a medieval joust. Both were wearing small venetian masks, which were required by the organizers, but even so, it was obvious how handsome they looked.

The ball already seemed like a big success; the lines in front of the tables collecting donations were three-deep. She looked around, searching for David or other friends whose costumes she knew about, but she didn't see anyone.

Then, at a table, she spotted a mermaid and a gondolier. She was sure they were Julie and David. Julie's costume was very fine and detailed; she looked very feminine, and somehow vulnerable. Even under the mask, the skin around her eyes looked a little puffy, so Nell assumed not everything was well at home. They were not touching, either; they stood close, but facing ahead and a little away from each other. In contrast, she and Jack were paired up in a half embrace. *Poor David is probably in the doghouse,* she thought.

When David looked up and noticed Nell and Jack approaching, he left Julie and, with the widest grin, first pumped Jack's hand and planted a big kiss on Nell's cheek.

"How are you, Your Royal Highnesses?" he joked, and either by design or accident, he still held Nell's hand in his.

Nell pulled her hand free and felt a slow blush creeping up her neck, so after greeting Julie, she excused herself to get some drinks, leaving the three of them talking.

She tried to find someone familiar, but she couldn't identify a friend. So she picked up a glass of champagne and started back toward their group. Jack was still there, talking to a handsome Poseidon, whom Nell identified as his friend from the hospital, Travis. Travis was the head of the laboratory at Jack's hospital, and he and Jack had known each other for ages. He was a little younger than Jack, but the two shared the same intensity, taste in sports, and political views, and they respected each other professionally. Travis was a very successful doctor; he frequently was asked to give his legal opinion or to speak at conferences, and he and Jack sometimes traveled together to symposia. They were in deep discussion about something, so Nell decided to go and check for her friend Shellie, who'd said she'd come as Snow White. The crowd around the donation tables was still too thick, so she walked toward the buffet to see what the food looked like. All the decorations and catering in the ballroom were very well done; no one needed to go hungry.

She decided against taking a plate, and was about to turn back when the "gondolier" found her. "Your Highness! I was looking for you," David shouted into her ear over the loud music and the noise of the crowd.

"I was afraid of that," she said, but was sure David didn't even hear her.

He grabbed her by the arm, took the champagne glass from her, put it on the tray of a passing server, and pulled her with him. *Where are we going?* she wondered. There were masked, laughing people everywhere, but David just pushed through the crowd purposefully.

Finally, they came to a smaller door on the side of the large room. David opened it, then pulled Nell through with him. The contrast was startling. It was quiet and warm here. It must have been a storage room. The organizers had left several boxes of decorations in one corner, and a sofa and a few chairs stood in front of an armoire in the other corner. The armoire held several dusty trophies lined up behind the glass door, which looked like they hadn't been moved for years.

As soon as they were through the door, David started to kiss her without any preamble or further talk. She felt herself being pushed back against the wall, the masks pushed up on their heads, lips locked and deliciously aware that their bodies were touching along their entire lengths. She felt the muscles under his costume, and had the strongest desire to caress and kiss every one of them. He felt so solid that she wanted to melt into him completely. His sexy smell invaded her brain; she felt herself being lifted and becoming weightless. His lips were exploring relentlessly, and she was dissolving like sugar in water. What a feeling! She'd never experienced anything even close to this before. She was aware of every inch of him, and the melting sensation was becoming stronger, hotter, and more urgent every second. His hips were pushing her even further, making her want to pull her legs around his waist...

She was sure she'd been waiting for this all her life: this complete abandonment of reality and the total thrill of their bodies being so close. She wanted closer contact, too! Were it not for the potentially tragic and frightening news of Jack's possible disease, the fact that they were in a public place, and the fact that David's wife was trying to get pregnant, she could not have stopped for anything. David was as lost in it as she was. He was slowly but surely exploring her skin under the costume, and she felt her fingers going under his shirt as well...

Finally she realized what they were doing. She knew she needed to put a stop to it right now. "No, David! We can't do this, and you know it!" she surfaced just long enough to tell him. "I told you, we just have to ignore our feelings for each other—"

"Baby, I can't deny it. We were meant to be together. I'm just so surprised that I didn't see it until now." With that, he resumed his attack on her senses and loosened another layer of her clothing, so he could have access to her neck and breast.

She didn't have any choice but to abruptly pull herself with the greatest force out of his reach. She could hardly stand up straight. She was panting, feeling both happy and furious—and a little lost. "Please, David! This is not the time and place!"

For the longest time, he just looked at her, not moving at all. Then slowly, he started to straighten his clothing. With a small, mischievous smile, he said, "You might be right, and I respect your wishes, but we need to talk about this soon." His eyes were so dark they were almost black, and they were shining most appealingly.

Finally she managed to say, "I hope you don't mean that what we just did was 'talking?'"

His laugh made her smile despite the circumstances. She started to make herself presentable, resisting the almost-unbearable desire to pull him back again for a mating that promised to be the most wonderful time of her life...

C'est la vie, she mused. *Finally, he notices me the way I was aware of him for a while, and now I have to refuse him...*

"Look, David. There are very important reasons that we can't do this now. Remember when you asked whether Jack was okay? Well, we're not sure. Jack might have a serious disease that will make him give up his work or possibly even kill him. We don't know yet, but if it's the reality, I'll have to stand by him, no matter what else I want," she said.

"I hope not, both for his sake and ours, baby!" said David, looking serious. "Because then my plan to take you away from him and keep you all to myself would be a very difficult thing indeed. How could I take the woman of a dying or seriously ill man?

"But you must know the truth, Nell. After some soul-searching, I've realized that I'm pretending to feel things I haven't felt for a long time. No matter how it turn outs—whether your situation will be temporary or long—I don't care. I'm going to have you. It's too bad it can't be now, but I'm a firm believer in instincts, and my instinct tells me this is the right thing for us. Don't worry, sweetheart, we'll make it work somehow! See you later!"

With that, he gave her a final peck on the cheek and stepped out of the room. Sharp, cold air swirled through the door and touched Nell's skin, raising a small shiver.

She finished putting her costume and hair back together, and followed him to the big room, where she hoped good news was waiting for her. She did not know it then, but her hopes were not going to be answered.

4

"It is so beautiful here!" Nell exclaimed as they walked down to the pristine beach from their private bungalow. Maui still had gorgeous and very private vacation homes catering to tourists who did not want to be in a crowd.

Their bungalow had everything: comfortable furniture, a collection of books and DVDs, even a private pool and spa—and no TV service. Their food was brought to them three times daily, and it was excellent. There were chaise longues and a few umbrellas on the beach. Their providers had even thought of UV protection, leaving several different kinds of high-SPF sunscreen in the bathroom. The bathtub was huge, lined with vials of baths salts and foams.

"But you're the most beautiful creature here! I'm so glad we came," said Jack.

"Thanks."

Jack sat down in the chaise, put his drink into the armrest holder, and waited for Nell to do the same.

They gazed out over the azure water and watched the sunset change everything to gold and then to orange. It was very tranquil, and it felt good not to be in the thick of things, yet she was surprised to feel that she missed it. Because she thrived on constant planning and running around to eliminate the next item on her to-do list, she felt this peace was more vacuous than truly relaxing. She knew she was a city girl. She just loved the hustle and bustle, the noises, the sights even—*horribile dictu*—the traffic. She loved driving, shopping, going out to dinner, dressing up...

None of that here. It was very quiet.

They needed to discuss the impending doom somehow, but neither of them could start the conversation.

Probably tomorrow, Nell thought.

They had dinner delivered, then made love and went to sleep—or at least Jack did. She was up until the wee hours of the morning, her mind running in circles about Jack, David, their kids, and all of the things that she had come to Hawaii to avoid thinking about.

In the morning she checked her phone and found several text messages from Chelsea and David.

Hi Mom, I miss u! wrote Chelsea. *When u come back I need to talk about the upcoming dance...*

I will be out of town, in Italy when u are back. Hope u have a great time, wrote David.

Reading David's text message reminded her again of the kiss, and she was surprised how vivid and powerful her memory was. Somehow she could not help comparing Jack and David, not only the different reactions she had to their touch, but their natures as well. Jack was a very calm, collected person, consistent in his intentions and solid in every way. David was more fun to be around and definitely more exciting. If Jack was like iced tea, refreshing and wholesome, then David had to be like champagne, heady and utterly enjoyable.

Maybe she was just an ungrateful, shallow woman who would never be happy with what she had. Maybe she should appreciate her good fortune more, her family and friends, and the lifestyle they had. She was trying as hard as she could, and for the most part it was working—as long as she didn't think about David and his kiss. The problem was that she was thinking about it even now, when she was having a romantic getaway with her loving husband. She'd read somewhere that men thought about sex every hour, and women only once a day, so she had to conclude that she had a caveman's brain, because it was on her mind almost constantly. Either she must avoid seeing David in the future, or their relationship would lead to sex. She had no doubt about it. That option was unacceptable, so she had to make sure that they stayed away from each other for a while. His trip to Italy was actually a very good thing.

The week went by, and Jack and Nell did have a good time. They both developed even tans and finished several good books by the end of the week. Somehow they avoided discussing Jack's health concerns; they mostly talked about Chelsea's future.

They also talked about how well Nell's business was turning out. She loved her fashion shops, and it showed. She was excited that her newest shop would be opening in Venice soon. She had an assertive, decisive streak that made her a good entrepreneur. Her real gift, though, was her fashion sense. Somehow she always knew which combination of colors, cuts, and fabrics would look good—both on her and her clients. Her store had unusual merchandise, including accessories that were a little more colorful and eccentric, but with her touch in putting outfits together, the final results were always very pleasing. She also loved jewelry, and her collection of unusual pieces made her store displays even more eye-catching.

Jack seemed in good spirits, and was also looking forward to getting back to his schedule of performing operations, checking on his happy clients, and seeing their daughter. Chelsea was a very well-adjusted girl, sometimes very strong willed, but smart and happy. He truly had a great family.

5

After returning to La Jolla, they got busy again. Jack was on his usually heavy schedule, and even though he looked a little more tired than usual, there was nothing else out of the ordinary. So Nell thought his fears about a serious illness must have been put to rest. One evening, she asked him, "Did you ever get those tests done that you were talking about? Do you still have symptoms?"

"Yes and no," said Jack. "Yes, I had some tests done, but they were fine. And no, since I'm rested now, I don't feel anything unusual. Don't worry, I'm still going as fast as usual."

For some reason, part of his answer didn't ring true to Nell. But at that moment she received a phone call about a delivery delay for the shop in La Jolla, so she had to end their conversation abruptly.

The next week, Jack seemed very upbeat and came home one night with flowers for Nell.

"What's the occasion?" she asked. "Did I forget an anniversary or birthday or anything else—"

"Hey, I just wanted you to know how much I love you, that's all," he said, and gave her a dazzling smile. He made Nell feel very guilty indeed, since she was still thinking a lot about David.

"So lovely of you!" She gave him a big kiss that ended up turning into something entirely different. He seemed strong, virile, and eager to please, as usual. Nell tried desperately to concentrate on their union and happiness together, but however hard she tried, David and his kiss never left her mind. Not for one second.

Jack began spending some quality time with Chelsea as well. They went together to the San Diego Wild Animal Park one afternoon, and Nell was pleased to hear from the conversation afterward that it was a great success.

One day, Jack announced he needed to fly up to Las Vegas next Wednesday to see an old friend. He said they'd studied together in college, and now Jack had a case he needed his opinion on. He said it would be nice to catch up with him after so many years.

Nell was sorry he wanted to go on the same day as her board meeting for the boutiques, but Jack promised he'd take her to Las Vegas some other time. He explained that it was the only day his friend Peter, who was a pretty busy man himself, had free.

"And what's his specialty?" asked Nell.

"Neurology," replied Jack, running down the stairs. "I'm taking the plane, so I have to call Thomas and ask him to prepare everything."

Thomas was the man at the airport who always took care of filing the flight plan and arranging for the maintenance of their private plane. Jack was an accomplished pilot, and even though keeping a plane was not a cheap hobby, his practice made it affordable. He loved to go on trips either by himself or with his wife. They had flown together to Las Vegas and Palm Springs, and they sometimes went to see his friends up in Napa and San Francisco. The plane was small, but had all the amenities and comfort needed for a family trip. Chelsea loved to fly, and sometimes even Sam, Jack's twenty-two-year-old son from his previous marriage, joined them.

Sam now worked in Los Angeles as a lawyer. He was a great guy with a good sense of humor; he always made his family laugh with his self-deprecating jokes. He and his dad were very close, talking on the phone two or three times a week. He'd lost his mother at the early age of three to a ruptured aneurysm, so Nell was his mom in any practical sense. He was compensated by the great family he'd ended up having. He and Chelsea adored each other, fitting easily into the role of brother and younger sister. Of course, he missed his birth mom, but he had been a happy child and was becoming a successful professional. Now, Nell wanted him to find the right girl, settle down, and have kids, but Sam seemed in no hurry.

Nell was a little worried about Jack's trip, since he had a sore throat. He'd spat up some of his coffee at breakfast, so Nell asked what was the matter. He'd said his throat felt scratchy, and he was probably coming down with something. But he assured her he was in good shape to fly. Usually he pulled through colds fast, so that put Nell at ease. It would be a short trip anyway, he said, as he planned to leave in the morning and return the same afternoon.

Nell would have a very busy day Wednesday, since all the store's finances had to be put on paper and she had to make sure all the legalities were followed before the scheduled meeting. She expected it to be a good meeting, since they were currently pulling in a 23 percent profit, which she thought was excellent. The accountant agreed.

Then she had to make plans for the upcoming store opening in Venice, which meant that she would have to go to Italy. That reminded her of David. He had an advertisement firm which listed some big fashion names as clients, so he attended the fashion shows from time to time. Nell had once gone with him to Milan for a few days. He'd had to work, but still had had time for some sightseeing and opera shows. She remembered that she'd been there at an ophthalmology conference, so it must have been some time ago.

In the last few days, he'd sent a few text messages and e-mails with pictures of Rome and Milan. She'd sent a short reply, but kept the tone general, like a letter to an old friend. David usually joked in his correspondences, but not now. She wondered if it was because he was busy there, or because he felt the need to distance himself, just as she did. Either way, it was for the best.

She missed him immensely, but tried to busy herself so she would not have time for such feelings. This plan had mixed results. Sometimes her nights were still steamy and sleepless.

I will get over this and it will be okay. She repeated her mantra and finally fell asleep.

6

She was exhausted and excited at the same time. They had almost finished the business at hand in the Wednesday meeting, and she was looking forward to hearing about the new line of clothing. Her assistant had put together a presentation to show everyone at the end.

"Let's have a coffee break, if you don't mind" Nell finally announced, unable to concentrate any longer. During the break, she decided to call Chelsea to see what she wanted for dinner and what time she would be home. She was about to make the call, when her cell phone rang, showing an unfamiliar number. She frowned, but took it. "Hello?"

"Is it Mrs. Jack Preston?"

"Yes."

"Ma'am, I am calling from the airport control tower at Las Vegas. We lost connection with your husband's plane about a half hour ago, and at this point we cannot see the plane on our radar. He hasn't contacted the San Diego airport either, so we're going to send out some search planes to see if he got into trouble. I want you to stay calm. We'll do everything to find him, and I'll let you know as soon as there is any development."

"Where was he when this happened?" she asked automatically, feeling a knot forming in her stomach.

"He was flying over the Mojave desert."

"Thanks. Please keep me posted."

She sank into the chair, and a single tear started down her cheek.

Kathy, her assistant, ran over and asked what the trouble was. She said dully, "Jack's plane disappeared above the Mojave desert."

⌒

They did not find him that day. It took three days before a search plane spotted something shiny on the ground.

The plane was gone. Jack was gone. They determined that the plane had sped down, almost as if there was no steering, and hit the ground with full force. It had exploded and left a little crater, some debris from the plane, and precious little of Jack. They didn't have much left from the plane, and it wasn't easy to determine if there'd been any mechanical failure, but they still did not give up the investigation.

Nell held up as she was supposed to. She was a strong woman, and she knew that she needed to be there for her family. Chelsea was devastated and wept for a long time. Sam kept himself together, but he was depressed and shocked. Nell felt too tired to answer questions and console others when she felt her self-control was slipping away as well. But she had no choice. She had to do it.

Now everything faded into the background except arranging the funeral and settling the estate. The cause of the accident was not yet determined. She told everyone that Jack was a great pilot. He took care of his plane and was very diligent in filing his flight plans, keeping everything in order.

The police came and asked questions about their relationship, the kids, possible affairs, and causes for depression. They insinuated that the crash had been no accident. She denied that possibility; he didn't have a reason for suicide, as far as she knew. She said Jack was a fighter and was not even slightly depressed. They asked if she had had any affairs, and she was immensely grateful that she could honestly say no.

David came back for the funeral, but because of all the visibility and her busy schedule, they only met for about a minute. He gave her a hug at the grave site, and then he was gone. Sam and Chelsea were at her side constantly. By the time the funeral started, even she was calm on the outside, so it went according to expectations. Jack had been such a good surgeon that half of the staff of his hospital had turned out, including his nurses and colleagues. Even some of his earlier patients showed up.

Even though she appeared calm, she felt like her arm had been ripped off. It was the most awful feeling. Finally it was over, and she went home and sat at her usual chair in their living room. She recognized the numbness she felt was leftover shock.

A few days later, she was sitting in the same chair, still feeling numb, when her phone rang. It was David.

"How are you, darling Nell? I wish I could help you somehow."

"I'll manage, but it's not easy. How are you?'

"Not so good. Julie is pregnant." He said it with a flat intonation. Even in her shocked state, she noticed the missing excitement.

"Aren't you happy?"

"Look, I am, and I'm not. I don't think we should have a baby now. You see, I don't love her anymore."

"Hey, I think a kid is always a blessing, no matter what. Are you staying here or going back to Italy?"

"I'm going back. I can't stay here. I don't want this, and I told her if she has the kid she'll have to take care of the baby on her own. I'm getting a divorce. Anyway...this isn't a good time to tell you all about this, but I head out tomorrow. Do you need anything? Can I help you in any way?"

"No, but thanks. David, are you sure about this?"

"About what? The divorce, yeah. The kid, no. Obviously, I want to be a good father, but I don't think it's a good idea to have a kid when a marriage is dissolving."

"What happened?"

"Nell, I think you know. I have to go now. I'll call you from Italy. Take care, love!"

And then he was gone. Just like that.

Jack is gone. David's gone, and tomorrow the insurance investigator is coming. Better get some rest if I can...

There was one thing that she hadn't done yet but that she needed to: call the doctor in Las Vegas. He'd left her a message yesterday, and after the expected condolences, he'd asked her to call back.

This is as good a time as any, she thought, and dialed his number. "Can I speak to Dr. Spector?"

"Speaking."

" Hi, I'm Jack Preston's wife, Nell. I'm returning your call."

"Mrs. Preston, I'm so sorry! I had no idea Jack would react this way to the diagnosis. Lou Gehrig's is a hard disease, but I told him he had a few years to finish his business and take care of things. He seemed very calm and collected, and I had no way of knowing he might harm himself. Or was it an accident?"

"Dr. Spector, what are you talking about? He said he needed to go to Las Vegas to consult about a patient. He didn't tell me anything about *being* the patient!"

"Look, he said I could share all the information about his disease with you, but no one else, since you were his family."

"What are you telling me? That he might have deliberately crashed in the desert because he found out he had Lou Gehrig's? But he told me he was feeling fine, he'd done some tests and they were okay, and he didn't have symptoms—"

"He told me he had difficulty swallowing, and I could already see some atrophy on his tongue. He had early-stage Lou Gehrig's, all right. It's a fatal disease."

"I know it's fatal, I'm an MD…although now I don't see myself as one, since I didn't even notice he had a problem. I noticed he spat up at breakfast the morning he left, but he said he had a sore throat. I believed him. Oh God!" Nell paused, stricken by a new thought. "You know, tomorrow the insurance investigator is coming. I'll have to tell him this, and then all hell will break loose."

There was a little pause before the answer came.

"Maybe you don't have to, Mrs. Preston. You see, we were very good friends from college, so I examined him at my home, not at my office. I haven't yet set up a file for him at my office. I've only shared this information with you. If they don't find a cause for the plane crash, they have to rule that it was an accident, and then you'll still have the insurance coverage for the plane. That's the least I can do for an old friend."

"But won't they ask you? You can't take such a risk on our account. It never even crossed my mind that he did it on purpose, but from what you said, it's the most likely scenario. Jack would never have wanted to waste away at the mercy of a feeding tube, dying slowly and without any dignity."

"Well, I can tell the truth to anyone who asks. Jack *did* have a patient to ask me about, so he had a real reason to see me. And the reason we were at my house is obvious, since we're old buddies. That's what I told the police when they called as well. Anything else going on in Jack's head was his own business. If you won't tell, neither will I. Do you know how much they recovered from his body?"

"There's nothing left to have an autopsy performed on, only some charred bone fragments. The plane exploded on contact and burned out with him in it."

"Then it's settled. It was an unfortunate accident. I'm very sorry for your loss. He was a great surgeon and a warm colleague. I think Jack would've wanted it that way. I'll miss him, and I feel for you sincerely, Mrs. Preston. In case you need anything at all, please just ask. I'll help if I can."

"Thank you so much for everything, I'll call if something develops or I have any questions, but I certainly appreciate your kindness."

With that, they hung up. Nell had been pacing, and now she sank slowly to her seat. She wasn't sure what to feel or what to think. In light of Dr. Spector's news, she was almost sure Jack had crashed the plane on purpose. Or had he? He was a very positive man who never gave up easily, but this had been a lost battle even before it started. No one could help you if you had Lou Gehrig's. It was a horrible death sentence, and he knew that for sure. First the muscles become weak, including the muscles that enabled swallowing and walking, so patients needed feeding tubes and wheelchairs. Later patients often ended up on respirators, becoming completely dependent on someone else to even exist. She was certain that such a life was just not what Jack would have wanted his last few months to be. He would not have tolerated dying slowly at the mercy of some nursing staff or some sophisticated apparatus that gave him another miserable, drooling month of existence. And in the end, she wouldn't have wanted it, either. Jack had been a fantastic man, and because of the way he went out of the lives of his loved ones, he could remain a strong and healthy hero in their memories.

She needed time to think, but before she could even get up, the phone rang again. It was Julie. "How could you!" Julie sobbed into the phone without preamble. "I can't believe I felt sorry for you after what happened to Jack. You were running around with David the whole time! How could you be so nice to my face when you were planning to take him away from me all the time?"

Nell could hear her distress rising, and tried to stem it. "I didn't plan anything! What are you talking about?"

"Like hell you didn't! He says he's in love with you and has been for a while and he doesn't want me anymore or my child..." She was crying again and taking in air with big gulps.

"Julie, calm down! I didn't hear of the separation until yesterday, I didn't know about your pregnancy, and I didn't have a clue he had feelings for me until a week ago! So please try to be reasonable! I was always his best friend and nothing more. David and I were never intimate with each other, I swear!"

"You know what, I don't care. If he wants you and not me, he's a fool! I'm the best wife I can be, I wanted to give him all my love, we were going to have a baby... and now this happens! I hate you! You can have David, because I don't want him anymore! You witch, you bossy old witch, I can't believe he wants you, not me..." Julie gave another sob. "Good-bye, Nell, and good luck to you both!"

With that, she hung up, and Nell was left to ponder two very important calls before the insurance investigator came around. At least now she knew her nascent relationship with David, if she could even call it that, would be a factor in the upcoming conversation. Julie had probably already spread the word and portrayed it as a fait accompli, so Nell guessed the investigator would have heard the gossip. She'd needed to acknowledge its existence to deflect suspicion. She was sure that even though the detectives had cleared her, the insurance agency would try their hardest to prove she was somehow involved in Jack's death, or that it was a suicide, so they wouldn't have to pay up the hefty benefit. It won't be an easy sell to convince them otherwise, but by God, she would try. Jack's decision was his own business. It was a good thing the investigator was a man, because she always seemed to earn more bonus points with men than with woman. For that she needed to look presentable, so she took a bath and went to bed. But sleep eluded her for a few hours still.

Before she went to sleep, she thought about how she'd never before recognized the problems in David's marriage. Now it was crystal clear that something must have been wrong. Why else would he keep a condo when he and Julie shared a big estate in Del Mar? Julie's parents were involved in real estate speculation and had done well for themselves. They had several large estates, and had given one to Julie and David. They mostly lived in New York and also had a property in Martha's Vineyard, where Julie and David went on vacation on their own or with her parents. David had said he needed to keep the condo for work because it was very close to his downtown office. He kept most of his travel necessities there, since he was in Europe a lot and sometimes in South America. If he was working on a project or went to a fundraiser and finished late, he just used the condo instead of going back to Del Mar. These facts were clues she'd never noticed before, but now they jumped out. It seemed he'd never really felt part of Julie's family, or that he wanted to keep some part of his life independent. That led her again to their kiss and how it felt, how she was craving it again—

Get a grip, woman! Poor Jack isn't even gone for a week, and you're already fantasizing about another man. Although he is the perfect one...

7

At eleven o'clock sharp, the insurance investigator arrived. He was a tall man with graying temples and blue eyes that did not miss much. He must have been in his fifties, but looked fit and healthy.

"I'm John Kendall, the investigator for Mutual Allied." His handshake was firm and he had a very sincere face. Nell thought he seemed like a fair and honest guy. "Under other circumstances I'd say I was happy to meet you, but even under these circumstances, hopefully we will part as good acquaintances. I'm sure you know the reason I am here. The question of possible foul play or suicide has to be ruled out. I talked to the detectives, and they gave me some information regarding their findings, but you're the one person who knew Mr. Preston the best and can shed some light on his mental state on this last trip. I take it that he's flown this plane on his own before, and there was nothing unusual about his trip to see Dr. Spector?"

"Yes, he's flown a great deal, for consultations or lectures. Various reasons. This was a normal trip for him, and I'd have accompanied him if not for the timing. He needed to see Dr. Spector on the day I'd scheduled my annual corporate meeting at my shop. I love Las Vegas, but I needed to be here for this meeting."

"Did he have any reason to be depressed or unhappy? Was he healthy? Either of you had an affair recently? Was your marriage working? I know these are a lot of questions, but we have to think of all the possible reasons for despair, loneliness, or a death wish."

"Yeah, those are a lot of questions. He seemed happy, I wasn't aware of any real unhappiness. I didn't have any affairs. I don't think he did either, but I never had it checked because I trusted him. He kept a good physical routine for himself, worked out, and aside from being tired sometimes, he seemed fine. We'd just come back from Hawaii, where we rested for a week. He was back at his hectic schedule and seemed to enjoy his work, as usual. Everybody loved him—the nurses, his colleagues, the patients, and his friends. I adored him, and I'm not aware of anyone who really disliked him."

"I talked to the detectives, the people at the airport, and some of his colleagues at the hospital," said Kendall. "They seem to agree with you that he was a great asset at the medical center and was very popular. From all outward appearances, everything seems fine, but as you know I'm looking for the not-so obvious. Do you mind if I take a look at his computer files? I'd also like to see the cell phone records for him and you and possibly other people to get a larger picture. Do you mind?"

"No, I don't. I don't have anything to hide. I don't think there was anything else involved except an unfortunate accident. He was a happy, fulfilled person. He didn't want to kill himself. I do understand that you need to verify all of this, and you need to see if anyone is lying or trying to give you false information. I will give you all that could be helpful; we don't want any delays or complications. So one extra tidbit of information I want you to know is that he had a sore throat when he started the trip. When I suggested delaying his flight, he told me he felt fine. Now I wonder if he didn't feel that good, and if that could have been a factor in the accident.

"The other piece of information I want to give you is about my cell phone record. You will see a lot of texting there between me and my best friend, David, who's now in Italy. We've been very close friends for almost twenty years now. I just found out from his wife, Julie, who is also a friend, that he's going to divorce her. She practically blamed me for the divorce and told me David is divorcing her to get together with me. I'm sure you can verify this if you talk to her. We were good friends, but I never had an intimate relationship with him."

"Were you aware of his feelings for you?" asked Kendall.

"Well, recently, he told me he had new kinds of feelings for me, but I'm very surprised that he's divorcing Julie," replied Nell. "They were trying to start a family, although David was not very enthusiastic, from what he told me. But I didn't realize the extent of his disillusionment."

"You said you were friends. Did you have similar feelings for him when you learned of his feelings for you?" Kendall probed.

"To be honest, I suppose I've always had feelings for David, but I discovered I had them only a short time ago. We shared a kiss at a ball, and that convinced me that the feelings were there. Although it's very unfortunate that the kiss happened almost at the same time as Jack's accident, there's no connection. I didn't intend to do anything about it, since I felt my family was more important, especially Chelsea, and I did not want to hurt Jack either. I think you can tell if I am lying or telling the truth, and if you need anything else to check up on, let me know. I want you to feel confident that you can decide fairly and correctly."

Nell saw him paying very close attention to her speech. He was checking out not only her words but also her body language. She felt confident that he was on her side and believed her.

"Well, it's certainly a surprise. I'll talk to this couple, and if you don't mind I'll check your text logs for some time back. I'll also ask your friends, and I'll tell you what I've found out in a few days. I do appreciate your openness about this issue. What's the last name of your friend David?"

"Nelson. He has an advertisement agency and travels a lot, so right now he is in Italy for almost a month, although he was recently back for a few days."

"How did you become friends?"

"We went to the same college and were swimmers on the same team. We never dated. I got married when Jack asked me, and he married Julie not long afterward."

"Look, I think I have what I need for now. I do appreciate your frankness, but I want to be sure. Did your husband find out or could he have found out of this change in relationship you referred to? Could he have heard about it from David's wife?"

"I think the answers would be no. I just found out about the divorce from Julie and David, and I think it came as a surprise to Julie. David never mentioned the divorce in connection to our feelings for each other. As for Jack, he believed in honest communication, so if he doubted anything even slightly, I'm sure he would've asked me first. He'd never kill himself over a suspected affair, he'd have confronted me. And as for the other side of this issue, I didn't in any way harm him, and I'm positive David didn't either. So there it is."

Then she handed him her cell phone, and he scrolled through the messages from the last few weeks.

"In case you want to see the e-mails, you can either view them on this phone or on my Mac, which is upstairs in the office," she offered. "I think Jack's was with him on the plane, so that's lost."

"That won't be necessary, thank you. I'm satisfied with these." He gave her a brief smile and stood, picked up his briefcase, and came close to her. "Thank you, Mrs. Preston. You were quite helpful, and I'm very sorry for your loss." By this time he was somber again, but Nell thought he still looked friendly. "I'll have to talk to the doctor he visited in Las Vegas. I'll be in touch." With that, they shook hands and he left.

Nell felt agitated. It had been a large step to talk openly about David, but she suspected Julie would have done it anyway, so it would've been futile to keep it under locks. Also, the information was a big-enough bone to chew on to distract from the other issue of disease as a reason for a possible suicide. She thought David would be unlikely to tell the insurance investigator about the possible illness, and no one besides him and Spector had ever heard about it. Although, now that she remembered it, Jack had said he'd done some tests. She remembered seeing him at the ball with his friend from the lab, so she made a mental note to find out about those results if she could.

Now she would just have to hope that it wouldn't be an issue anymore. In any case, all the little pieces of the puzzles didn't prove anything. Nobody would ever know exactly what had happened. She suspected that Jack's friend was right, and he'd crashed the plane on purpose, but that was just speculation. There was no reason to drag Jack's reputation through the mud and hurt his loved ones over her suspicion.

Now that she was alone again, the whole affair started to weigh on her. She missed Jack and all the security that he gave her and Chelsea. Now she and her daughter needed to fend for themselves. *Correction*, she thought, *now I need to fend for both of us.* Then she thought of Sam, who must be pretty down himself. Maybe in time it would feel a little less painful. With that she called it a day, and after giving Chelsea a little support, went to bed.

8

David called her cell phone the following morning. "Hi, sweetheart, how are you? I wish I could be there to support you, but I assume your family needs time alone anyway. It's a horrible blow to lose someone after so many years. I'm so sorry, baby!"

"Hi, David. You have no idea how difficult it is to hold it together, not to scream and shout, for Chelsea's sake and for the outside world. On the surface I'm calm, even when I was talking to the police, to the insurance agent, to Jack's colleagues, boss, everybody. But on the inside, it's very sad, exhausting, and frightening. I've never had to organize a funeral, grieve, and try to console everyone else, all at the same time, even though I'm hurting as well."

"How are Chelsea and Sam doing?" asked David.

"Sam's holding up. I was worried about Chelsea, but she seems to be handling it as well as can be expected. She's in shock, but she's still taking care of her everyday responsibilities. Her rhythm is still intact. The same can be said about me as well. We just have to go on, since there's no other choice.

"At least I've got a support system. I get so much sympathy, everyone feels my pain a little bit. But…maybe the only person who doesn't feel sorry for me at all is Julie. She called and told me she hated me. She blames me for the divorce. Are you sure you want to go through with it now she's pregnant?"

"We'll talk about it when I get home," replied David. "That's why I called. Looks like I need to stay here in Italy for another month. One of my biggest customers is throwing a party I've got to attend. Will you be all right without me for so long, sweetheart? I wanted to come see you now, I'm so anxious!"

"It's okay, David," said Nell. "Maybe it's better that we don't talk for a while. I need time to mourn and be alone. And you need time to rethink this divorce. Don't be impulsive!"

"I'm not being impulsive, I've made up my mind. I don't love her anymore, and I can't pretend. Not even for the sake of children. It wouldn't be fair to either of us. Look, I'll see you as soon as I'm back." His tone changed, becoming lighter. "Sweetheart, please wait for me, and don't accept any marriage proposals, okay?"

David always joked with her, but this comment had a new edge to it. Nonetheless, it still felt good to be teased by her best buddy, and for just a few minutes her problems seemed to be less heavy. "Aye, aye, sir," she teased back. They hung up.

Nell was relieved David would be out of town, since she needed to wait for Chelsea's sake anyway. She also wanted to hear her best female friend's take on her romantic thoughts about David. She trusted Shellie's opinion despite her not-too-perfect track record with relationships. *People always see others' problems with more clarity than their own struggles*, she thought.

In the next few moments, Nell caught herself in yet another erotic daydream involving David. She stopped herself, and wondered if something was wrong with her. A widow's sexual fantasies about her best friend only days after the funeral should not be a regular or acceptable thought process. She felt terribly guilty, but she still couldn't help herself. David's handsome face and hands were on her mind. What a mess! How did it happen? How did a nice, safe, low-key admiration change to out-of-proportion longing and full-fledged suffering? She wanted him to be here, right next to her or even closer. In a few weeks he would be here, and still she had to play it level-headed and cool about this consuming, raging lust. Then the guilt came again. *How can*

I think about another man when Jack, my husband of so many years, has just been put in an early grave? I must be a monster! Heaven help me!

Nell reflected on their phone conversation. She'd deliberately left out her discussion with the insurance investigator. That way, David could tell his side of the story the way he wanted to, with no secrets, no surprises, and no withheld information. She was fairly certain David would not mention Jack's suspected disease, and since the divorce was an independent—although a very conveniently timed—event, he would make her statements stronger by confirming it to the investigator.

Had it been a suicide? She found the question haunted her. Perhaps it hadn't been; perhaps it had been a momentary lapse of reason or carelessness on Jack's part because of all the things he was mulling over. Who knew? There would never be a definitive answer, as the investigators at the field could not determine the cause. At least it had been fast and hopefully painless. By the time the flames came, he'd been dead, and for that she was very grateful.

～

The next day, she'd just come home when the phone ringing made her jump. "Hello?"

"Hi, darling! How are you coping?" It was Shellie, her long-time friend. She sounded so upbeat and pleasant that Nell was already looking forward to seeing her.

"Can you come and see me a little later? Or maybe we could go somewhere to have dinner?" she asked.

"Hey, why don't you just come over to my house and we can order some Chinese food and just talk a little."

Shellie had a nice house on Coronado, right on the beach. They usually went out to walk on the sand after dinner when they ate at her house. "That sounds so healing! I'll see you in an hour?"

"Sure! You can bring Chelsea if she feels like coming."

"Thanks, see you then."

Nell called Chelsea and asked if she wanted to accompany her to Shellie's place, but Chelsea said she'd promised Michelle that she would go to her house after swimming. She said she would watch a movie or read and then go to bed early. It sounded like a good plan, so Nell let her go. She picked up her bag, changed her dress to a pair of pants and a black T-shirt, and walked out the door.

The one thing she still enjoyed, despite of all of her troubles and sadness, was driving. Her Cobra was a real beauty; she just loved to feel its power under her. She started to analyze herself again, reflecting that her love of fast sport cars seemed at odds with her feminine style. Loving sports cars was so typical of men. Although, more accurately, she loved Mustangs and Cobras. Those were the only cars she ever bought; she just adored them. She assumed it was somehow a part of her personality—the part that was very assertive—that made her love the same things men loved. Luckily for her, she was very far from masculine in appearance, but her likes and dislikes often followed those of the stronger sex. So despite the incongruities, she was grateful for her pushy, aggressive attitude; it was the basis of her professional success. And it was probably the reason she was such a good match with David, at least in terms of his mental processes and business practices. He was a very successful man, not only because he was a hard worker, but also because of his mantra that there were no impossible tasks, only difficult ones. She felt drawn to that mantra herself, although she knew she just used it as an excuse sometimes to prove a point. She loved to feel she'd created a done deal, accomplished a task to everybody's satisfaction. She was resourceful and relentless, just like David. They both ran tight ships in their businesses.

Driving over the gorgeous Coronado Bridge, she looked at the fantastic sunset. It took her out of her grief, and she thanked her lucky stars for the millionth time to live in such a fantastic place. San Diego was a bustling, vibrant city, beautiful beyond anyone's expectations. There were still nice things in her life, after all.

9

Shellie was a vivacious golden girl, born and raised in Southern California. Her light-blond mane was always a little unruly, and she always had a few freckles on her short, pretty nose. She'd finalized a second divorce about six months ago, and finally felt back to normal again. She was irrepressible, optimistic, and loved to laugh about anything.

But today she was somber and gave a hug to her best friend at the door. "How are you, sweetie?" She used terms of endearments with almost anyone in sight. Her mom called everybody "darling" or "precious," so that was probably the origin of her habit.

Nell plopped down on the overstuffed white sofa, already feeling relieved. It was very relaxing to be with Shellie. They'd been friends for over twenty years now, since they'd first connected at school. *Wow, that makes me feel pretty old*, she reflected. But it was the truth.

"I'm as fine as I can be, I think. I miss Jack. And I miss the normalcy of my time, the regular schedules of things, if that makes any sense."

"Of course it does. How are Chelsea and Sam?"

"Considering their loss, they're doing very well. Very depressed and sad, but going on with their lives. Jack was a great father."

"He was a good guy. A great husband, a great doctor. It must be tough for the medical center to lose him, too."

Nell mutely nodded, and they sat in silence. Nell felt like sobbing, but she stayed quiet, reaching out to her friend for comfort. They hugged for a long moment.

Finally, Shellie spoke up. "You said you wanted to talk about something very important and shocking."

"Yeah, I'm kind of afraid to even tell you about this." Nell hesitated. "It's so unexpected, I have a hard time rationalizing it to myself."

"I want to hear it. You know you can tell me anything."

"I'm in love." Nell let out a breath she didn't know she'd been holding. "And I just found out about my feeling for this guy before the accident. Nobody knew about it, probably not even him. Jack had no idea. Hell, I had no idea until the kiss."

"Wow, that is shocking! What kiss? What guy? Tell me everything! It must be very recent, since I had no clue, and you say that Jack didn't know either. Were you going to act on your feeling or try to suppress it? I can imagine both responses from you without any problem. Gosh, I'm sorry, it must be even more difficult to handle everything this way."

"I can't tell you how long ago I felt there was something more than friendship there. It must have been months—"

"Oh no! You're talking about David, your best friend, aren't you? Does he feel the same way about you?"

When Nell looked at her and nodded, she stopped asking questions. "Well, go on. Sorry for the interruption, but it *is* shocking!"

"So, just to make a long story short, a few weeks ago, when we went to that fund-raiser, David and I shared a kiss. That's when I knew for sure what I felt for him was much more than a regular friendship mixed with a little crush. The strangest thing about the whole thing is that I didn't have any problems at home with Jack, at least not that I'd noticed. I thought we had a very good marriage and agreed on most things in life. We saw the future the same way, we loved the kids, you know that.

"Anyway, apparently David had some feelings for me, too. I thought that he and Julie were getting along just fine, but he didn't seem very happy with the pregnancy program. Then at the ball he kissed me and said something about finally realizing he had feelings for me. I told him to cool it, and I had no intention of acting on my instinct to start a relationship. It was probably the hardest thing I ever did, considering I almost died of desire right then and there, but luckily I still had some of my higher-brain functions working as well as all the base instincts, which were going full throttle. He left, and I hoped that would be the end of it, despite what he told me before he left. He said he'd pursue me and wouldn't give up so easily. Then he left for Italy, and we didn't talk much. Then the accident happened to Jack, and within a few days I was mourning my husband and arranging a funeral." Nell paused, unable to go on.

Shellie's jaw dropped. "Wow, I'm blown away!"

"I was hoping for a little more detailed analysis!" Nell managed to give a half smile.

They settled in for a long discussion, covering her friendship with David, Julie's pregnancy and angry phone call, David's divorce, and the insurance agent's questions. Nell wrapped it up with, "Now I worry about all of these factors and I feel extremely guilty, even though it was all a coincidence. As I'm trying to sort this out, I realize that I'm in love with David. I was blind not to see it earlier. It looks as if he's had the same thing going on for some time."

"At first I was surprised, but if I think about it now, I probably shouldn't be," said Shellie. "I always thought you and David looked like a very handsome pair, and you really were very close. Not that I gave it a second thought, since both your marriages seemed to be going well. As it turns out, one of those marriages was an illusion. If the turning point for realizing what you felt for both of you was that kiss, it must have been one hell of a kiss."

"Shellie, it was. I can't tell you anything else, just that the whole world disappeared from under me and I felt a connection so basic, it was almost frightening and delicious and thrilling and—"

Shellie put her hands up and interrupted her with a characteristically broad grin. "Hey, I get the point! Yeah, it certainly seems something major must have happened to the two of you. I hope I'll have that kind of kiss someday, but after two failed marriages it's doubtful I'll ever get there. Sorry, I know this isn't about me, we're talking about you. But I still start to fume every time I think of Paul and his ways."

Shellie's husband of five years had been found cheating with a student at UCSD, and she was still very sore from the experience. Their divorce went almost normally, with no big disputes or fights about property, but Nell thought that Shellie's trust in men was probably shot for a long time.

"I'm sorry, I reminded you of your ex. I don't think that was very nice of me."

"Come on, sweetie, don't even waste a thought on that jerk. Let's have some dinner and we can talk further after that."

They ate take-out on the deck, watching the sun over the water. They both loved Chinese food, like walnut prawns or orange chicken, but they seldom indulged. Tonight was a much-needed exception.

After they'd finished, Shellie said encouragingly, "You know, I always thought David was an outstanding guy, very successful and likable. And you two are amazingly similar in some aspects. Like his interest in animal rescue. You remember how he spent two months somewhere in a remote animal center to help mustangs? I know you're crazy about them as well, and you're always trying to do something for animals and for preserving our wilderness areas. I always thought it was very interesting how you two seemed so similar and liked the same people, had interest in the same charities, both swam, and both were so successful at your businesses."

"Thanks, Shellie. That makes me feel a little less crazy," replied Nell.

"And I always wondered how he could end up with Julie," Shellie continued. "What a spoiled little rich girl. She was nice to look at, but it ended there. I was never able to have a real conversation with her. She seemed vacuous somehow. Although she was always so focused on David, almost like a rolled-up red carpet waiting to unfurl to serve her master. Maybe I'm being a little harsh. Well, anyway, I never liked her."

"I didn't care her for that much either, but because of our outings together with David, I spent a lot of time with her and she considered me a friend. I felt like a mother figure to her; she always seemed to be lost or unsure of things. Well, either way, it seems like she's out of my life."

"And David is in, big time. Were you really going to just ignore your feelings after the ball? And what would you have done if Jack were still here?"

"Hard to say. But I didn't have a plan after the ball. Despite of all of this, I loved Jack. I'm completely confused and surprised by my feelings. You know how cerebral I am about almost everything. This is the first time in my life that I feel my primitive self taking over, and no matter what my cortex says, I'm charging down a path I don't even want to take. Or do I? Well, you know me, so I'm sure you understand what I'm trying to say."

"I do, but I have to tell you that I envy you, for lack of better word. To feel so strongly about anything is a precious experience, even if it's awfully painful too."

"You should have been a therapist, I swear!" exclaimed Nell. "That's exactly how I'd characterize this mess I'm in. What I'm surprised about, though, is that you've never felt this way. I thought you were completely in love with Paul at the beginning."

"I thought I was, but I still had all my cortex functions involved, all the little manipulations and plans," answered Shellie. "I was very cerebral about the whole thing. The abandon you talk about was never there. Ever! I didn't miss it, since I didn't know it existed, but seeing you now makes me long for it. I hope someday I'll find a man who makes me feel like you do for David. And—my God—I can't imagine how you'll be after you have sex with him! I bet you'll be walking on air...I'm sorry, I shouldn't joke about anything right now, should I?"

"Don't worry about it. You should say what's on your mind. I need some normal interaction. The last few days I've heard nothing but condolences, and it makes me even more sad instead of giving me any comfort. I still feel like I have a hole in my soul. So...what's your advice on what I should do?"

"Go for it! If you feel it and it feels real, it'll be worth all the troubles. I think you and David will be a very well-suited couple."

"But what about Julie and her pregnancy? Everybody will think I'm a horrible witch, not only to forget my wonderful husband so fast, but to take the husband of a pregnant woman."

"Is this for you or for the public? Come on, you know better than that. The people who can't handle you finding happiness aren't really your friends, so forget about them."

"And what about Chelsea? I need to talk to her soon and see what she says. I just can't go ahead with this if she sees my future relationship as a betrayal toward her dad."

"I agree, I think you should wait and talk to her. But I seriously think Chelsea and Sam will understand in the end. They've always loved you, and it's obvious you'll be very happy with your new mate; I can see it through all that sadness and sorrow you are carrying. So shush! You deserve to have happiness, especially after what you went through just now. David will be good, not only for you, but for Chelsea. And I think he'll get along with Sam just fine."

"I hope you're right!" said Nell fervently.

"You know I'm always right! Except, of course, when selecting my own husbands."

With that they settled down, watched an old romantic movie, and went to bed. Just as Nell drifted off to sleep, she thought about how nice it was to have friends like Shellie.

⌒

At six, she was up, and they went to the beach to walk for a half hour. They talked about Shellie's plans. She said she was going to Mexico for a few weeks and would call as soon as she was back. She was getting some supplies there for her antique shop. Her little store was always stocked with things from Mexico and South America.

Then they said good-bye, and Nell headed back to see if Chelsea was doing all right. She arrived just as Chelsea was about to leave for school, and she came through the door and gave her daughter a big hug.

"Mom, I'm so happy you went to see Shellie! I can see she made you feel a little better."

"Yes, love, it was nice. And I need to talk to you about something as well, do you think you might have some time this afternoon?"

"Sure, Mom, I'll be home around three. We can talk then, okay?"

"That sounds great! Love you!"

When Chelsea had left, Nell looked after her a little anxiously, fearing the subject of the afternoon talk. She did not plan to broach the subject of her feelings for David, but she wanted to tell Chelsea about David's divorce. She knew it would not be an easy conversation.

Still, when the talk finally came that afternoon, it was easier than she'd expected. Somehow Chelsea did not seem very surprised. She didn't even ask about the reason for the divorce, so Nell thought she was probably still in shock over losing her dad. Originally, she'd wanted the two of them to go pick up Jack's ashes, but the conversation convinced her that Chelsea's wounds were too fresh for that. So she went to the funeral home alone.

When she came home with the ashes, she could not help talking to Jack one last time. She put down the beautiful urn, sat, and had a mute conversation with her beloved husband. *You know, I loved you and I was so lucky to have you in my life. You gave me the biggest present anyone could give. Chelsea is a terrific daughter, no one could wish for a nicer, brighter girl. I also love Sam. He's just like you in so many ways. I just feel so sad you won't see your grandkids.*

Love, I have to tell you about something that might shock you. I think I've fallen in love with David. And if me seeing him doesn't make Chelsea too unhappy, I think I might end up having him as the man in my life. I hope you'd understand. You were always so level-headed and practical. I really think you would approve. I'm very sad we parted this way, so I couldn't tell you one more time how wonderful you were. You will always be in my heart, you know that.

Good-bye, my love. Rest in peace.

With that, she closed a huge and important chapter in her life. As happens so many times in life, she just had to move forward, however hard that might be. That was what she needed to do.

Despite all her good intentions, she had a few very miserable weeks coming up. She missed David so much, felt completely alone and desolate, yet she had to pretend normalcy and business as usual for everybody's sake—and for her own as well.

10

David was tired of his trip. He wanted to go home and see Nell. It seemed like the last few weeks had been crawling along at a snail's pace. He'd received news of Julie's first sonogram, which showed a healthy fetus, and that made him a little happier. Despite their separation, he wanted to have the little baby. He was sure Nell wouldn't mind. She already had two terrific kids.

As for the rest of his stay, it had been pretty bad. He went through the motions, but could not really concentrate on anything. Now that he realized he loved Nell, he couldn't seem to contain his desire to be near her or contact her somehow. He sent her a few text messages and called her, but most of the time, he got her voice mail, not her. His patience disappeared. Not that he was a patient man normally, but this was unbearable.

Fortunately, today was his second-to-last day in Italy. He had to endure three meetings and one party, and then he'd be free. The party was in honor of a very big client in Milan who made most of his travels to Italy worthwhile, so he had to attend. Mr. Palazzi had a large business, and he relied exclusively on David's agency for his advertising. He was a nice gentleman, and had a beautiful wife and a daughter. The daughter, however, was a problem; she'd had a crush on David for the last year or so. Camilla Palazzi was a striking beauty with dark eyes and rich mahogany hair so thick it had to be braided to pile it on her head. She looked like a Madonna from a Renaissance painting. Her fingers and neck were long and elegant, and she had a killer figure. She'd set her sights on David, and he couldn't simply brush her off without jeopardizing their account. Camilla was Daddy's little girl, spoiled and used to getting her way.

As soon as he stepped into the magnificent salon, which housed probably a hundred very well-dressed, rich, and important guests, she came over to him and latched onto his arms. "Oh my! You look so sexy and handsome tonight," Camilla murmured into his ears.

"You look awesome yourself, Cam!" She was wearing a blue satin dress that didn't leave much to the imagination, and which gave a good account of her considerable assets. She knew she was sexy, and her posture and movements made sure everybody noticed it.

He tried to steer them toward her father, hoping she'd refrain from hanging on him so obviously under her parents' eyes, but it was not an easy job. The crowd was thick and loud. Laughter and music came in waves, and after almost every step there was an offer of refreshments or hors d'oeuvres from the well-trained staff, who glided between the throngs.

He took two glasses of champagne, handed one to her, and pretended to drink from the other, toasting her beauty. She downed the drink in one gulp and was already looking for the next one when he got lucky. Giuseppe, her father, found them and gave David a big handshake. He told Camilla that he needed David for a few minutes, and steered him to a group of older men. Camilla was not happy and seemed to be pouting, but she knew her father well, so she gracefully let go of her gorgeous American. Giuseppe introduced David to the gentlemen, who were considering using his agency in the future, so David had to answer questions, exchange cards, and act like a good rep for his company.

When he finally got free, he saw an opportunity to sneak away in the form of another acquaintance, a fashion photographer. The man was leaving and asking for his coat, so David said he'd like to have a word with him and stepped out of the salon to accompany him. David had seen him before at another client's fashion show, and so they chatted about the upcoming schedule for David's other big client's show next week. David said he was sorry to miss the show, but asked the photographer to send him a few pictures to see how it went.

At the street level, he pumped his hand, got into a waiting taxi, and went back to his hotel. He just did not feel like playing Camilla's games tonight. She was attractive all right, and she was also willing to give him anything he wanted, but now was not the time. It was not a good policy anyway to mix business with pleasure, but it had sometimes happened to him before. Now his only objective was to fly back and seek Nell out. He wanted to convince her of the seriousness of his intentions, that they belonged together. He was afraid some other man would offer his services to her before he could make his move. Nell was very admired by many men, and with Jack gone, David was sure they would come out of the woodwork. Even though he believed Nell had the same feelings for him as he did for her, it was better to be safe than sorry.

After taking a quick shower, he slid under the covers and went to sleep almost immediately.

He woke to a movement next to his legs, and when he turned his head, he was shocked to see Camilla next to him. She was smiling at him and pushing the covers down, and after seeing his eyes open, she revealed her round, perky breasts right next to his chest. "You have a very cute birthmark on your bottom. I'd love to kiss it if you let me."

"What the hell are you doing here, and why are you naked? Cam, what's going on? I didn't invite you here, and I want you to leave now! How did you get into my room?" David pulled back the cover and, naked as he was, jumped out of the bed and went to fetch the robe from the bathroom, covering himself on his way back.

"I have my ways. It's a nice habit to sleep in the nude. I like that about you," said Camilla without making a move to leave the sheets. Now she was stretched out completely naked for him to see, with her dress lying on the floor next to the bed, along with the shoes and underwear. She did not seem to take the hint, probably thinking that David wanted to play a game.

"You have to go! *Now!*" he said, but she still did not get the message.

"Come on, baby, you can't tell me you don't want me, I've just seen your erection. Why not come here and play with me a little?"

"Because I don't want to! And as for my hard-on, it's the morning, so I would have it regardless. C'mon, Cam, you're a beautiful woman, no question about it, but I won't have you. I won't embarrass myself or your father—who, by the way, would be very disappointed to see you offering yourself like this. So please just go and forget about this!"

She finally understood his rejection was serious, and a slow blush began to creep up on her neck. "You bastard! You'll be sorry!"

With that, she took the garment from his hand as he was offering it to her, jerkily put it on, and after casting one more venomous look in his direction, she left, banging his door so loudly that the whole level must have heard it.

This day is starting out just great, he thought. His flight to the States was in two hours. He put his things in his suitcase, and right before he left the hotel, noticed a text from Nell. *I've heard a gondolier will arrive today. We need to talk when u arrive. I will call u.*

See u later, Your Highness, he texted back.

With that, he got the porter to collect his luggage and left for the airport. He had no idea that the day was far from finished. It would reveal even more surprises—not very good ones, either.

11

When he arrived home, David noticed several missed calls from Giuseppe. He assumed he'd forgotten to discuss an aspect of the new ad campaign, so he quickly called him back. To his complete surprise, he only heard shouting on the other end of the line. "What did you do, you bastard? You wanted to rape my daughter? I'm going to the polizia! You'll be sorry you ever crossed my family!"

"Giuseppe, please, what are you talking about? I didn't do anything to Camilla! She came over to my hotel room without invitation!"

"So you admit she was there!" shouted Giuseppe. "You thought it was all right to slap her around and try to force yourself upon my sweet daughter? I trusted you with my business, with my family!"

"Please, I did no such thing," said David, feeling dazed. "I told her to leave, because I didn't want to take advantage of her. I didn't touch her at all!"

"Then how do you explain the torn clothing, the finger marks on her face? She came to me in such a state! She knew about your birthmark—if you weren't naked, how would she know? As of today, I'm withdrawing my entire account from your company, and I'm going to the polizia. You won't get away with this!"

With that Giuseppe hung up, and David was left with a growing sense of doom. Even though he was innocent, he had no way of proving it. As far as he knew, no one had seen their exchange. It had been pretty early in the morning, so most guests had still been in bed when she left. Maybe the hotel attendant at the front desk or the taxi driver had seen her leaving. Although, if there were finger marks on her face, someone else must have been involved. She could have torn her own clothes, but it was doubtful she'd slapped herself. She'd probably paid a few people to back her story up.

Losing those accounts would hurt his company, but it would be a far bigger problem if he could not prove his innocence: he'd be considered a criminal! At least he was back in the U.S., and he could try to figure this out without going to jail. He had a friend who was a private detective in L.A., so he decided to give him a call. Then he would call Nell and tell her, before she heard it from anyone else.

He sat down to his desk, opening the computer to check if there was anything in the Milan papers about Camilla's story. Her family knew a few editors in that town as well, but David hoped they wouldn't go down that road, since it would be probably very embarrassing to the family. He never would have thought Camilla could pull such a stunt.

The phone suddenly rang. It was Nell. He took it. "Hi, tiger! How was your flight?" she asked.

"Hi, sweetheart! The flight was fine, but now I have a problem I need to talk to you about. Can I see you soon?"

"I need to see you too. I got a call from Travis, and he said he wanted to see me tonight. He was a colleague and a friend of Jack's, so I want to talk to him, but our schedules have clashed for the last month. But I can cancel, if you'd prefer."

"Tomorrow might be better, in that case. Although I missed you so much, I'm very tired and look pretty beaten up. So if it's okay with you, let's meet tomorrow so I can impress you with my looks as much as with my wits. Do you want lunch or dinner or both?"

"Hey, I would love both, but I have to work tomorrow until about three, so let's do dinner. You want to meet at the restaurant or at the condo?"

"Meet me at my place at six, and we'll decide there. I need to tell you something important, so it might be better to stay in and order take-out. I miss you so much!"

"Looking forward to see you, handsome!"

Nell was almost relieved to have an extra day to deal with things other than David. For one thing, she needed to find out what Travis wanted. Before that, though, she wanted to see if Chelsea had time to talk. She knew she couldn't delay telling Chelsea about the situation with David. *She's a big factor in what I'll be doing,* she thought.

She anxiously waited for her daughter to come home. When Chelsea showed up, she was wearing a pair of black jeans and a simple top. She looked like a young woman, Nell noticed. There were many boys interested in going out with Chelsea, but she was still seeing Ryan, her first boyfriend of two years. As far as Nell knew, they'd only necked and kissed, which was a relief. Nell had emphasized to her the importance of using protection in case she did have sex, and she was sure Chelsea would remember. Nonetheless, she hoped her daughter would wait until the act would mean more than a check mark on a to-do list.

"Hi, love! How are you today?" asked Nell.

"Hi, Mom. I'm okay, considering..." Her red, puffy eyes showed Nell that she had been crying.

"You want to talk?"

"Why don't we just go to my room and listen to some of Dad's favorite music?"

"Sure. But before we go, I need to tell you something. Sit down, love." Nell paused. "David is back from Italy, and I'll see him tomorrow. I wanted to talk about him. What do you think of him?"

"What do you mean? I like David, he was a good friend of you and Dad's for a long time. Is he okay? I hope this isn't about some bad disease or something. I don't want to hear more bad news for a while…" Chelsea's voice trailed off.

"No, it's not that. I have a hard time telling you this, so I'll just come out with it: David and I like each other as more than friends."

"What?" Chelsea seemed dazed. Nell, afraid her daughter would next erupt with accusations or throw something, put up her hands and said, "Please, let me finish, so I can explain. I never had anything going on with David, so this isn't about us having an affair behind your father's back. As a matter of fact, if your dad were here, it wouldn't be an issue. We'd still have our old life, and I would never have brought this up.

"The whole realization was very recent. It happened right before the accident. David and I shared a kiss, and we both realized we had feelings for each other. I told him that I'd ignore it, but David was already unhappy in his marriage, and he told Julie he'd divorce her.

"Then your father crashed, and we lost him. I loved your father very much, you must know that, but I wanted you to understand. If you see me and David getting together now, that's the reason. I wasn't going to act on this feeling. We had a strong family, despite what I felt for David. I don't know if you believe me…or do you hate me for telling you this?"

For a long time, Chelsea didn't say anything, but looked at Nell intensely. Then she spoke. "I could never hate you, Mom. I believe you would've stayed true to us despite David. You must be in love with him, otherwise you wouldn't bring it up so soon after Dad's funeral. I know you loved Dad, and I know you love me very much. We had a very good family and I'm very sad it's shattered.

"It's hard to deal with, but in some ways I can understand your situation. You know, I *am* sixteen, so I notice things more than before. And for a while now, I've been wondering about you and David being so close, always so happy together. I was sure David was thinking about you. Somehow, I felt it. When the four of you were together, it was always just you, Dad, and David. Julie was somewhere else, or she just seemed like the odd one out, so I had a hunch. I didn't think you were having an affair, but I was… worried about the future."

Nell put a hand on her daughter's back, silently reassuring her. Chelsea continued, "Mom, I love you, and I want you to be happy. If David's going to be the man in your life, I understand. I just wish Dad was still here."

With that, the tears started to fall, and Nell rushed to hug her. All the pent-up sadness and anxiousness welled up in her, and she started to cry too. "Thank you, love! I had no idea that you were so mature and forgiving, but I do love you for it."

They sat there crying for a while. Then they went to Chelsea's room to listen to some of Jack's favorite songs. They reminisced about their good times together as a family. A phone call from Michelle interrupted them, and Chelsea agreed to join her friends for an old movie. She left, and Nell got ready for her meeting with Travis, putting on a simple but pretty blue dress.

As she drove to the restaurant, she felt an enormous sense of relief and gratitude. If Chelsea had reacted differently, Nell reflected, she'd have tried to break things off with David. She'd have tried to get him out of her head. Maybe she would have been unsuccessful, but she'd have tried for Chelsea's sake. It was much, much better to have her daughter's support and understanding.

It might still shock most people when they found out about her getting together with David—but she was sure now that it would happen.

12

When she arrived at the restaurant, Travis was already there. He was dressed in a smart pair of khakis and a green shirt. He looked fresh and expectant.

They picked a quiet corner table so they could talk. After ordering their tea and club soda, Nell looked at him curiously. "I'm so glad that we could finally get together. I can't believe he's gone. I know you and Jack were very friendly colleagues, so it must be hard for you too."

"Yeah, it won't be the same without him at the medical center. Everyone misses him." Travis cleared his throat uneasily. "You must be wondering why I wanted to see you, so here it is: Do you think Jack might have had a disease? Jack asked me to run some lab tests for him. He asked me specifically about signs of muscular atrophy or degeneration. At the ball, I gave him the short list of the results. They were inconclusive, but there were some signs of muscle problems, nothing specific. He said he'd injured himself exercising, and was feeling more tired than usual. I guess we both decided there was nothing to worry about.

"When I heard what happened, I was as shocked as everybody else. I just hope I didn't miss something in that lab report that caused his accident! I rechecked the report and I couldn't find anything, but I have to ask you too: Do you know anything more about this?"

Nell spoke carefully. "Well, now that you mention it, I remember he had a recent lab checkup. When I asked him about it, he said that he felt a little run-down, probably because of the heavy workload. So we took a vacation.

"When we came back, he felt fine and looked completely healthy. The only thing I remember is that he had a sore throat when he left for Las Vegas. I told him to stay, but he wasn't about to postpone a consultation for such a minor thing.

"As for the injury, I'm not sure, but he mentioned he pulled his deltoids at the gym. He said it was sore for some time. He didn't mention that he had signs of muscle degeneration—that's what you said, isn't it?"

"Well, not even that," replied Travis. "It's just that he had a higher level of an isoenzyme, which is usually a sign of muscle injuries, diseases, heart problems, nothing specific. I just felt I need to at least check with you to see if he had anything else going on. Was his heart all right? When was his last checkup?"

"Last year they had him do the stress EKG, and he also had a scan of his coronary functions. The results were excellent. He took care of himself. Maybe it was the muscle injury that caused the elevation?"

"It could very well be. Look, I didn't mean to make your mourning harder, I just thought I would see if you knew about it. It was probably just the shoulder injury."

With that, they veered off the subject of Jack's health and did not come back to it for the rest of the dinner. As they parted that evening, Travis took her hand warmly. "Now that Jack's not at the center, we might not see you and Chelsea anymore. It'll be tough on an old fox like me. If you need anything, I'm here. Just call me. I hope we won't be strangers."

"Of course not! I still expect you to keep sending me those fundraiser invitations! I might go to Europe for a while, just to get away, but when I get back, I'll call and see if we can work together as before."

Nell drove away, pondering their conversation. She assumed that Jack hadn't wanted Travis to suspect anything; why else would he have lied about that exercise injury? She'd backed him up because she knew it was what he would have wanted. That meant that no one, except Dr. Spector and Nell herself, knew definitely about his illness. It also meant that Jack had already suspected his diagnosis from the lab results. Had he wanted to spend time with both her and Chelsea before he went to see the neurologist, because he knew he was going to kill himself? That was a big bite to swallow, but she was more and more inclined to think he'd crashed on purpose.

The thought made her feel terribly guilty. *Should I have guessed it? Should I have intervened? Probably not, but if I knew, how could I resist?* Jack had seemed so calm and collected, so full of energy. On the surface he'd been an efficient, happy surgeon, a great husband and dad—but all the while he'd suspected that he had a deadly disease. Not only that, but perhaps he'd planned to end it and leave everybody without even saying good-bye. Nell realized this was a side of Jack she'd never known about. She would never have believed it, but now it was right in front of her.

That brought her back to another issue, namely David. How could she have been so blind to their mutual attraction, when even Chelsea had noticed it ? Something must be wrong with her; she was missing things left and right. She'd considered herself a very perceptive person—until now. She'd also failed to notice David's marital troubles, when even Shellie had thought David and Julie had a weak marriage. Maybe deep down she'd had the same opinion, but she'd never really considered or stopped to analyze it. Not that it would have been her business, but it would have been a warning of what was to come. She hadn't stopped to analyze her own feelings for David either; she'd just assumed it was a close friendship peppered with a little lust. Way off! She knew that, if this "thing" between her and David worked out as she hoped it would, it would be the best of the best. Despite all of the misgivings, the heartache, and the sorrow, she could hardly wait.

She arrived home, took a shower, and got under her quilt in her favorite satin gown. She closed her eyes and pretended it was David who was touching her nipples, already eagerly showing through her gown and deliciously rubbing against the quilt. It was enough for her just to think about him to get aroused. She thought about their kiss again, and the memory raised goose bumps on her skin. She remembered how David had pulled her head close and cradled it with his hand, how his erection had strained against her belly, how his fingers had left hot marks on her ears and a delicious tingling wherever they made contact with her skin. How his tongue explored every part of her mouth, her lips almost sizzling from the sensation and the pleasure spreading down her spine, the whole weightlessness of it. His unbearably delicious touch on her breast and neck, which made her mind blank to everything except the desire to be taken by him.

She was still surprised that she'd had sufficient presence of mind to halt it when she had. And the only possible future was to pick up where they'd left off and go all the way. She wanted him with a desire unknown to her previously; it was so overpowering that it frightened her. But would it stop her from moving forward? Impossible. She had to have David, there was no question about it. She could hardly wait.

Then guilt about the whole affair set in again, so she jumped out of bed. She drank some milk, and decided to call it a day. After tossing and turning, she went to sleep.

13

The next day, Nell couldn't stop thinking about her upcoming meeting with David. She felt both anxious and expectant. She was not sure if anything physical was going to happen, but she had a feeling all over her body, a kind of restlessness and a premonition of something leading to a basic change, something dramatic and exciting. She wondered about the problem that David had wanted to talk about. She'd felt even on the phone that he was a little nervous about this subject. Was it a general misgiving about their union or future together? Probably not. David usually didn't worry about other people's opinions. If he made a decision, he just acted, everyone else be damned. His willingness to take risks and be different was a big part of his business success. *Well, I'll find out soon enough*, she thought, checking her jeweled watch for the sixteenth time.

In the meantime, David had been checking all the possible newspapers in Milan to see if Camilla Palazzi was mentioned anywhere, but he didn't find anything. So far, so good. He called his friend and asked him to find details that could discredit the story so he could clear himself. His friend had been in the detective business for decades, and was now a successful private detective in L.A. David had done some favors for him in the past, so now was the time to call them in. Franco promised he would get right on the case, and though David offered to pay, Franco remembered the past and insisted he'd work pro bono for his old buddy. Since he was a second-generation Italian, Franco spoke Italian fluently and had several connections in Italy. It seemed like a good start.

David felt a little better after the call, and he also thought the fact that the Palazzi family was silent about the case was a good omen. Maybe even they were wondering about Camilla's far-fetched story.

He selected his clothes carefully, opting for soft, dark blue corduroy pants and a shirt he remembered Nell complimenting him on before. It was light blue, covered with small white spirals. He had to agree with her; the shirt looked very good on him indeed. He always had well-made Italian leather shoes, so it was a given she would like those. She would also, hopefully, like the man in the outfit.

He couldn't help remembering when he had almost ravished her in that airless little room at the ball. She was everything a woman should be: sexy, beautiful, and exciting. Just thinking about the way she'd grabbed him under his shirt made him hot. She'd definitely been willing, and had wanted him as much as he wanted her. Until she'd decided it was not to be finished right then and there, she'd been so passionate and eager, exposing herself to him so that his blood boiled. What he remembered the most was her hips undulating against him and her hands going into his hair, her fingers massaging his scalp slowly. The sweet taste of her mouth, the way her eyes went completely dark, her expression of complete abandonment and desire...*I need to think of something else*, he decided.

He was worried about how Nell would take the news of Camilla. She had known him for so long; surely she'd believe him. Thinking about their twenty years of close friendship reminded him of the strangeness of the present situation. How had he never noticed that he wanted her before? That was the strangest of all the questions. Obviously, he'd always thought that she was a very sexy woman. He'd admired her for both her looks and her personality; sometimes he'd even lusted after her a little.

But she'd never gotten to him as she had last month. It was far deeper and more basic than anything he'd ever felt before. It was almost frightening, considering they'd only kissed and nothing more. Every minute he was away from her, he felt as if he were on autopilot: going through the motions, but not really there. He wanted her to be next to him, to see her radiant smile and hear her laugh. And most of all, he wanted her to touch him again all over. *Here we go again*, he thought. He decided to call the office, for no other reason than to distract himself and think about something other than Nell.

She came in bringing colder, fresh air with her, and she took his breath away. She had on a sun-yellow short dress with white embroideries on its hems and sleeves. Her matching bag and high heels were white. She wore a little lip gloss and very minimal makeup. She looked and smelled fantastic.

He pulled her into his embrace and was contemplating never letting go, but eventually came to his senses. After giving her a light kiss on the lips, he led her to the settee. "So, how are you, beautiful?"

"I've been better, but we're going to be okay. It's just so hard to have your family break into pieces. I manage, the kids manage, but it's still very difficult to feel such a loss."

"How are the kids doing?"

"Chelsea is still pretty down and even though he doesn't show it, I'm sure Sam is depressed as well. He was here last week for a few days, and we shared some memories of his childhood. I am sure he'll miss Jack terribly. The one thing that I am happy about is that he seemed to have found a very nice girl, and has been seeing her for some time now. How about you?"

"I've been better, too. I really am sorry about Jack. He was a great guy, and we all miss him. I'm glad that the kids are coping," said David, then took the plunge. "Look, I'm having some problems. One, of course, is the divorce from Julie. I had no idea it was going to be at the same time as Jack's accident, which will make people suspicious if we get together. You know it's a coincidence. On the other hand, I'm serious about it. I've realized that I don't love Julie, and that I want you more than I've ever wanted any woman in my life. I refused to stand aside and let our mutual attraction not be answered. When you were with Jack, I know you didn't want to act on it, but I bet I could have changed your mind. It's a moot point...but now I have the opportunity to pursue you in the open and with all the ammunition I've got. How do you feel about that, love?"

"I want you to pursue me! I want you to want me! Despite all of the horrible loss and all of the sadness, that's the one thing that makes my days bearable—that you might still want me. Do you really?"

Without another word, he took her into his arms and started kissing her again the way she remembered. She felt herself melting completely again and had the irresistible urge to touch every part of his body, feel every inch and millimeter of it. She was hot and tingling everywhere, her skin coming alive under his caresses. If there had been fire when she mated with Jack, this was fusion! And their bodies were not even fully touching; they were both fully clothed. *I must have died and gone to heaven*, she thought.

"Wait, we need to talk first!" This time it was David breaking the contact and pulling himself back. He panted, then said, "I'm sorry—or should I say, I'm not, but I couldn't help myself. You were on my mind constantly, and I want you so badly. But I need to tell you about something awful. I really hope you'll understand and trust me."

She felt a little fearful, but nodded to let him know she was listening. She was still out of breath and wanted more of David, but she had to be a friend first. "Just come out and tell me. You're going to marry someone else? What else could be so awful? I can't imagine anything about you that I wouldn't approve of—"

"Well, it's a story about me that's not true. But it's awful, and I want you to know about it from me before it gets to you another way. I was accused of raping someone in Italy. I have this large account with the Palazzi family in Milan, and they had a party before I left. I was invited and spent some time with the daughter of my client, Camilla. She's very young, and for some reason she had her eye on me as her future husband. I did nothing to put that notion into her head, I assure you. So I was nice to her, but I left the party pretty early to avoid her. To make a long story short, I went back to my room early and since I was tired, I slept like a log. When I woke up, Camilla was lying naked under the sheets with me, and since I always sleep naked, she got a pretty good view of me before I woke up. This is important, since she later told her father that she had seen a birthmark on my butt, as proof that we weren't dressed.

"As soon as I woke up, she told me she wanted me to make love to her, and certainly made it clear that was the reason for her surprise call. I wouldn't have done it, even if that was the strongest desire of my life—I didn't want anything to do with her and her wedding plans. So I jumped out of bed, put on a robe, and asked her to leave. I asked how she got there, and she just laughed and didn't answer me. She first thought I was just teasing and didn't mean what I said, but soon she realized that she'd made a mistake. I made her put on her clothes and leave. On her way out, she threatened me, but I didn't pay too much attention.

"But when I got back to the States, her father called me and claimed I tried to rape his daughter, slapped her around, tore her clothing. He said he'd report me to the police, though I haven't seen anything in the papers, so I think they're keeping it to themselves. When I tried to deny it, he told me that Camilla even knew the place of my birthmark, so we had to have been naked. Her clothing was in shreds, and she had marks on her face as if someone had slapped her around. Someone must have helped her with her story, because I certainly didn't slap her or tear her clothes.

"I have to clear myself. It won't be easy, because I'm not there. They have all the connections and they know the system there. I underestimated Camilla, I just had no idea she would pull a stunt like that out of spite. I have a friend in L.A. who's a private investigator, and he's going to find out if anyone saw her leaving my room with her face and clothing intact. I didn't do anything to her, I swear!"

"I'm so sorry, David!" said Nell. "That certainly is a bad ending of a good business trip. I believe you, I don't doubt for a second that's what happened. I'm just afraid you might not be able to prove it, though. I hope your friend is good and can get things done abroad. Otherwise it's not an easy task."

"He's good. He's fluent in Italian, and he has a lot of connections there, so if anyone can dig up the facts, he can. At least I hope so. Thank you for trusting me! You know, I shouldn't be surprised that Giuseppe believes his daughter, since they're a close family, but it's still very hard to take. I've been called lots of things I deserved: a heartless jerk, a womanizer, a cold-hearted bastard. But none of those hurt like being called a rapist."

"You're not a jerk, David, and you're *certainly* not a rapist."

"So you're still willing to stay with me for dinner, then?"

"Sure, you cold-hearted womanizer."

They decided to go out to eat at the water, so they went to the Top of the Cove in La Jolla. They had a very nice and relaxing time and caught up with the recent changes in their lives, discussing other family matters and some business developments. She was absorbing some of it, but was mostly looking at his gorgeous face and wishing they'd finish dinner and go home soon. She was sure David was completely innocent of the charges the Palazzi family had brought against him, but could not help feeling a few sharp jabs of jealousy thinking about Camilla. The fact that she had seen David naked and knew about his birthmark somehow made her feel furious. The bitch! She couldn't wait for the moment when she would check that birthmark out herself...

14

On their way back to his condo, Nell felt herself getting suddenly nervous. It was a very unusual feeling for her, because she always was so relaxed around David; that was why they always joked and never had fights. He was just the easiest person to be around, and she felt completely at ease whenever they were together.

Not now! She felt her palms getting a little damp and her mouth going dry. If she hadn't know better, she would have called it stage fright. She'd felt this way before her first business presentation—and before her first time with a guy, for that matter. Roger had been his name, and though he hadn't been a very sophisticated man, the fact that he was her first had made her uptight before the act. It had turned out to be very "nice"—at least that's what he'd called their union afterward. She'd enjoyed it very much and agreed that it was nice, in spite of her nerves.

Roger must have liked the sex as well, because he'd wanted to marry her. That had been her first marriage proposal, almost twenty years ago. She might even have married him, too, except that the previous day she had met Jack and felt herself drawn to him immediately. Roger was nice, but Jack was so sexy and magnetic. She knew there was much more to him than Roger could ever hope for. He was a widower and immediately showed interest in her, asking her for a date at their first meeting. She'd refused Roger because she'd felt Jack would turn out to be the one that she was waiting for. And he had been.

Back then, David was still changing girlfriends more often than most people change their socks. Now, looking at his gorgeous profile, she was still completely surprised: how could she have missed the connection they had? His looks were probably part of the problem. He was *so* good looking that he was considered a pretty boy. Nell loved handsome men, but frowned upon the pretty ones. She should have looked under the surface; they were friends for a reason. He wasn't just classically attractive, he was dependable, funny, well educated, very intelligent, well-read, and considerate. He was also very giving, which she considered a rare quality in men. Usually, they only cared for their families, their wives, or their girlfriends. Not David; he did a great deal of work for several charities. He had lots of friends, both male and female, and he gave them gifts, wrote them cards, and went to lunch with them. He had several very good friends from his college days and he still kept in touch with them, going out with them to games, concerts, or car races. He was equally comfortable with his female friends, and if he were not definitely and very positively male, he could have been one of the girls. He never forgot a birthday, and he was constantly calling, texting, and sending funny e-mails to his friends. He was a social animal, for sure. She loved that about him.

Now that she thought about all of this, she realized that she loved almost everything about him. His straight nose, his well-muscled chest, his hair, and his hands. She was already imagining them on her skin, traveling up and down her spine. His lips were full and his smile was out of this world. And he had a butt to die for...

Get a grip, girl, she thought. All her anticipation was balled up in her midsection somewhere. *Grip or not, I want him so much, it almost hurts...*

She noticed him sneaking some sideway glances, but the drive was mostly quiet, almost unnaturally so. *Is he feeling as nervous as I am? But he's a man, and has so much experience with women.* Before he'd settled down with Julie, he'd played the field. As far as Nell knew, he hadn't cheated on Julie during their marriage, and she was pretty sure she would have heard about it both from David and from other friends who knew them well. Still, the fact remained that he could make a lot of comparisons, and her experience was very limited indeed. She couldn't help wondering if she would measure up.

David parked the car, and then they were on their way up in the elevator. He put his arms around her shoulder and gave her a little peck on her cheek, almost like a feather. "You know, after what I told you, I understand if you don't want to stay with me. I want you to, but it's entirely up to you. So tell me how you feel."

"David, you know I want to. I could try to lie and tell you I'm not interested, but I am. I'm so nervous, I can hardly speak—"

"Nervous? Why? You're the most beautiful woman on earth, and I want you more than anything. Is it because of the Italian affair? Sorry, wrong word—you know what I mean."

"No, it's not. I told you, I trust you completely. I'm also all set to check out your birthmark myself."

She stopped, and was surprised at his laugh. He pulled her to him and planted a kiss on her mouth that promised fantastic endings to come.

"If you kiss me like that, I won't be able to put one sentence together. No, I'm just a little put off by the fact that I've been with very few men, and I wonder if you'll find my experience lacking. I'm more excited than I've ever been in my life, but I feel like a teenager, not too sure about my way."

"Don't worry, my love, I'll show you the way, and I'm sure we'll be fantastic together. Usually, for me the sex came first and then sometimes I had feelings for the lady later, but that happened only a few times. Now it's the other way around. I have feelings I never felt before, and I know we're great together as friends, so I'm positive our sex life will be out of this world. I hope we'll be having one?"

"Hey, no pushing! I'm so happy that you're confident about everything, I just feel a little unsure, that's all. I guess I just want to impress you so much."

"You already did that, babe. So no worries. We'll get to enjoy ourselves, you'll see."

They were at the door, and he let her go in first, but did not turn the lights on. Instead he pulled her into his embrace and started to show her what he meant. Despite her misgivings, they found their rhythm very soon, and shed clothing all over the floor on their way to his bedroom.

She was so taken by his beauty and physical perfection, she didn't even have time or space to think about her fears. In the dim light, she thought he looked like a Greek god, powerful and dangerous. His muscles were hard and his skin smooth under her palms. It felt absolutely wonderful. She touched him everywhere, and from his expression and his moans she was sure that she could please him immensely.

She was glad about the dimness; she was still worried about her trouble spots and felt a little unsure about her nakedness, but he seemed to like her the way she was. Looking into his eyes, she felt beautiful and all-important, not to mention the feelings that his touching evoked in her. Wherever he caressed her, she felt a hot trail and a good kind of shivering overtaking her. When his kisses went lower than her neck, she felt she was floating.

"I always knew you were beautiful, but I still couldn't have imagined how much! You're definitely better than any of my fantasies about you," he said huskily.

"I didn't know you had fantasies about me." Her voice sounded alien to her, but she loved his comment because it made her feel a little more comfortable in her skin. Looking at his expression, she was sure that he meant what he said.

Then they started to feel each other everywhere, and the experience was unnaturally pleasurable. For her, it was better than any of her fantasies about David. He took his time, even though she was so aroused that he could have taken her in the elevator. They did fit perfectly, she thought, before her mind all but disappeared in the sensations.

By the time he actually took her, she was flying and never wanted to land again, ever. He was not only inside her body, but her mind, her cells, her whole being.

She heard him calling her name when he came, right after she started to see prisms of flashing lights. It was absolutely amazing for her, like nothing she'd ever experienced before. She felt him expand into her every pore, and a feeling of belonging pierced through her pleasure. To call it exceptional would have been a gross understatement.

Afterward, he very gently cradled her and gave her small kisses. She thought he was probably trying to help her feel secure and forget her previous misgivings. Or he just wanted it that way. Either way, she was very grateful he was doing it.

"You know I love you, don't you?" he whispered.

"Well, that's a very nice thing to say, although the statement comes at a very suspect time," Nell answered. "But I appreciate it anyway. I think I love you, too, tiger. I'm just so surprised that I had no idea all these years we could end up together."

"That means we need to do more catching up, love." He was nibbling on her ear and her neck, getting her excited again.

"Wait, you didn't tell me if I got a good grade or not! Was I better than your other ladies, or at least like them?"

"You're way ahead of any woman I ever had, babe, so stop worrying and start giving me some serious loving instead."

After a few kisses, he asked her, "How did you like my birthmark, by the way?"

"Mmm, I loved it, it doesn't only look good, it tastes good, too. I also loved your scars." She traced the marks on his hand and forehead. "How did you get those?"

David remembered her caressing and kissing every millimeter of those marks, and wanted to skip the talking altogether, but she pulled herself back. "Hey, I want to know!"

"Okay, the one on my hand I don't remember much about. I was a kid, and I was playing outside. My mom says I fell on a piece of broken glass. The one on my forehead was when I went deep-sea fishing with my friend in college. I slipped on the deck and ended up splitting open my forehead. It's still crooked, since I never got stitches. It just healed on its own. Now, I can also remember I had a tick once, and his bite mark must be somewhere near my groin. You want to give me a kiss there too?" He pushed her head to the area and was pretty happy with her compliance. "Yeah, somewhere around there, baby! And now it's my turn to see if you have any markings..."

~

They played until the dawn started to color the windows pink. She was just too damn high on endorphins to worry about a thing. She was sure her brain was simply overloaded with dopamine and serotonin. She knew this because she was completely happy— almost unnaturally so.

Nell had never really been interested in philosophy, but she had to think about how improbable it was to feel so important and invincible, when in reality they were such little specks of living matter, floating somewhere in an immense universe in which they did not even register as small. "Small" were stars, galaxies, black holes. She couldn't envision the universe in its scope, but even its "small" components were immeasurably beyond her scale. Compared to them, what was she?

But here and now, she felt like she and David had created a universe for themselves, a moment of complete bliss and belonging. How weird was that? Even weirder was that it was all achieved by tiny molecules playing tricks on soft, pink, living computers, all in order to replicate themselves. Because she was sure that was the reason for all their happiness and the unstoppable force that had drawn them together: it was simply biology at its best. Their genes just wanted to capture the future, so they could float as newer specks in their descendants and do it all over again, procreating and surviving. That was why sex was so enjoyable; if it wasn't, who'd go through the trouble of pregnancy and child rearing? Sex was the bait, survival of the species the hook.

She was sure that she was losing her mind as she thought about all of this now. She was also sure she wanted to spend the rest of her life with David. The only question was whether he felt the same way. *Well, we'll just have to see, won't we?* She fell into a dreamless and contented sleep in the arms of her perfect lover. For the first time in weeks, she rested well.

15

She awoke, and for the first time since the funeral, she was aware that she didn't feel terribly depressed. David was looking at her with quiet adoration in his eyes. "I hope you didn't mind spending your night with a rascal like me. I certainly had the best night ever, despite your 'inexperience...'"

That brought a blush to her cheeks, as she remembered what they'd done close to sunrise. She'd thought Jack had been intimate with her, but now she knew there was another level of intimacy that she'd never even known existed. David had explored her body at every possible angle and depth, giving her the opportunity to do the same with him. It was a novel, exhilarating experience.

He was touching her now, trying to excite her. It was working. "Don't you ever have enough? I usually got less sex in a month than I did last night. Looks like we won't have much time for conversation if we get together, tiger."

"It's impossible to have enough sex, especially if you're with someone so utterly desirable as you are, love," said David. "I think I'm in love not only with you, but with your nose, your ears, breasts, legs..."

"Stop listing all my body parts, I'm a whole human being, if you didn't notice. And for your information, tiger, my sexiest organ is my brain."

"Okay then, let's fuck your brains out, sweetheart. Are you game?"

"I don't approve of bad language, you know that. On the other hand, you turn me on whatever you say...so let's do it!"

After another hour they were all sweaty and spent. She realized that they needed to start their day, so she gave David another kiss and told him she needed to go. "I'm not sure I can walk to the shower, but I have to go take care of some business. I think you need to work a little too, no?"

"Can't I just sleep instead?" he asked, smiling up at her wickedly.

"Well, it's your business. I have to run some errands and drop in at the store, and then I need to be with Chelsea."

"Okay, I have some work to do as well. I also want to check if anything came up in Milan. Can I see you for dinner?"

"I don't see why not. You're addictive, tiger."

"I certainly hope so, love!"

With that they took a shower, got dressed, shared a nice kiss, and parted for the day.

Nell couldn't remember the last time she'd felt so light and happy. She understood now what "walking on air" meant. She was doing it today.

She was afraid Chelsea would feel bad about her spending the night with David, but her daughter showed no outward signs. They had to do some shopping together to decide on a dress for the upcoming dance. Chelsea admitted she felt a little guilty thinking about her dress and having fun only weeks after her dad had been put in the grave, and they almost broke down at the store together.

"You know your daddy would've wanted you to enjoy yourself. I think he would tell you to do that if he were here with us," Nell managed to say, but was on the brink of tears herself. She felt very guilty about her happiness and all the erotic images popping into her mind throughout the day. She considered herself sometimes to be a hedonistic, shallow bitch, a monster—and yet, other times, she thought there was nothing wrong with the happiness David brought her. Being torn about anything was new to her; usually, she made up her mind about things and just ignored the doubts. This time it was a harder than usual.

They did end up buying a dress, and it seemed to be a good choice, showcasing her daughter's beauty. It was turquoise, made of a silk-and-synthetic blend that did not wrinkle. It was short and had a simple cut with a square neckline. Chelsea looked terrific in it.

Nell couldn't get images of David's anatomy out of her mind's eye all the way back home, and didn't pay much attention to Chelsea's phone conversation with Michelle. She heard, though, that Chelsea would stay the night at Michelle's. Since she trusted Chelsea's friend and liked her family, Nell didn't mind.

Throughout the day, David also had visions of Nell from time to time, and it put a smile on his lips, sometimes even making him hum some of his favorite tunes. He was unquestionably happy and was looking forward to seeing her in the evening.

He called Franco in L.A. The investigator had collected some information, but nothing that would change the standing of the case. He hadn't heard of any hotel employees who'd seen Cam leaving David's room, nor had he found the person who had let her into the room yet. Franco told David not to worry; he'd find the truth. The polizia must have been notified, because there were some detectives asking the same questions of Franco's connections. The investigator said that was a good thing, since whoever had helped Camilla might realize this was more serious than a bad practical joke. Eventually, they might be intimidated enough by the investigation itself to tell the truth.

David wanted to believe him, but had a sinking feeling about the whole affair. He'd hoped a guest or employee would back his story up, because he knew the family would always believe Camilla. Not only were they proud of her, but on the surface, her story made sense. Even he would have given it some consideration if he were part of her family. Hell, she could even report the size of his erection, despite the fact that he'd never intended to do anything to her. Telling about his birthmark was a master touch, indeed. It was on the middle of his buttock, so no one could have seen it unless he was naked.

He cursed himself for having slept so heavily that night. Normally he was a light sleeper. If only he'd woken when Camilla had entered the room! Although he wasn't positive, he suspected she'd wanted to have sex and then get him to marry her. To her young mind, it might have seemed easy to manipulate him, given that her father was such an important part of his business. She was beautiful and rich, so in her mind, she had everything going for her. David was still amazed by the sudden turn of her mind, how easily her little scheme had turned into spite and revenge. He certainly hadn't expected it from Camilla. *Well, somehow we just have to deal with this and get to the bottom of the story, that's all. Easier said than done…*

Just to make his day a little lighter, he sent a text to Nell and also ordered two dozen long-stemmed roses delivered to her home. They were her favorite color, coral red. For the card, he decided on "For the woman of my dreams. I can't wait to see you again! Love, David."

16

Chelsea left for Michelle's house, and Nell started to dress for her evening with David.

She finally chose a coral-red dress, the same color as the roses she'd received earlier in the day. The dress accentuated her nice décolletage and gave a good view of her phenomenal legs. She matched her strappy silver sandals with a silver purse and dangling earrings of the same color. At the last minute, she grabbed one of her black, expensive blazers in case it got cooler, and stuffed a fresh pair of underwear and transparent hose into her purse. Then off she went to see her lover.

After arriving at David's condo, she saw Shellie had called her cell phone. Since David was not there yet, she called her back.

"So, how are you?" asked Shellie. "Is David back from Italy? If yes, tell me what happened!"

"I'm well, and yes, he's back. And yes, what you predicted happened: I'm walking on air!"

"So you slept with him! Wow, how was it?"

"Indescribable and out of this world! If I knew it could be like this, I wouldn't have waited until now to experience it, for sure. I really can't tell you how it was, because I'm lost for words. Now I'm positive that I'm in love with him, and from what I've seen so far, he might be in love with me as well. Who knows, it might even work out for us!"

"Not to repeat myself, but wow! What do you mean, it *might*? It'll work out, I feel it in my bones! It'll be the best marriage ever."

"Wait a minute, I was talking about love, not marriage. That's not the same thing."

"I know, but I'm sure he'll propose soon. Although it must have been very recent, since he only came back yesterday. Did you do it at the airport or what?"

"Come, on don't be nasty! I didn't even see him the first night back, only on his second one. We did it at his condo, and if I'm right we'll do it again today as soon as he comes home. I'm waiting for him here."

"Did he do anything romantic after you slept together?"

"Yes, he did something really nice, he sent me two dozen roses in my favorite color and a beautiful note. Do you think that's a good sign?"

"Definitely! Nell, he'll propose in a month. Mark my words, you're going to be a bride soon!"

"I think you're full of it, and anyway, I have to go, because I hear the elevator coming up. He'll be here in seconds. I'll call you tomorrow."

"Bye, and remember what I said!" Shellie hung up, and Nell wasn't sure whether to laugh or to take her seriously. It must be her romantic nature, but she couldn't help hoping it would actually happen.

She did not have more time to muse before David came in with a dazzling smile. He seemed tired, but incredibly sexy and handsome. He wasted no time. "Hey, you're certainly a sight for sore eyes, darling. You look ravishing, so can I ravish you?" He came over and started to demonstrate what he meant, but Nell pushed him back a little.

"Wait just a minute, handsome! I want to hear if you found out anything about Milan, then you can tell me how your day went, ask about mine, and then you can start ravishing."

"Too much talking, babe." But he complied anyway. "I didn't hear anything promising, my day was okay, not very productive, and I hope your day was nice. Now, can we get back to touching, finally?"

But she still pushed his hands away and said, "Thank you for the beautiful roses, they made my day! They were fabulous! I also had a nice time with Chelsea, and I'm very grateful she isn't resentful of us, despite the fact that she misses her dad terribly. She's so kind to me! We got her a dress for a school dance that she was hesitant about going to, but I told her Jack would surely want her to go enjoy herself, so she decided to. Okay, *now* you can give me a kiss."

Between kisses he told her about his conversation with the insurance agent, and confirmed he'd given the same explanation of events as she had. "I told him that I realized recently I had serious feelings for you, but I didn't even have time to do anything about it before Jack crashed. I also told him about my impending divorce, and I even told him it was because of you.

"You know, I really am sad. I liked Jack, and just because we would've been adversaries over you doesn't mean I wanted him harmed in any way. I hope that insurance agent doesn't get wind of this thing brewing in Milan. It'd make me even less trustworthy in their eyes. A rapist—I don't even want to think about this."

"Maybe I can make you forget…"

Nell started to unbutton his shirt until he stopped her and said, "Help me with taking off your dress. It's very nice and looks fantastic on you, but right now I want to see you without it, please."

"Yes, master! Any other instructions? I'm more than happy to please you in any way I can."

"Well, let's see. How about checking me for tick bites? You can never be too cautious."

"I thought you went to the office, not the outdoors," she teased him back.

"Yeah, but you know, it's a jungle out there."

Teasing, playing, loving, smiling, touching, and exploring consumed the night. She was more relaxed and more willing to venture out of her comfort zone, and he showed her ways to feel even more connected and satisfied. She tried to map out his every inch, his every smile, his expressions and all his mannerisms, and put them into her memory for good.

They were seeing different sides of each other. Even though they'd known each other for almost a quarter century, they'd never seen each other naked—and not only in the literal sense. They were more vulnerable, more intent, more intimate, and more willing to see each other without normal barriers.

It was surprising to Nell how hard it was to relax and not to try to impress David. Somehow, she wanted to be perfect for him. It was tough being in front of another person without pretenses and conventions; to show herself as she was, and risk being judged.

She'd never had these scruples with Jack. Somehow, Jack seemed to worship her from the beginning, and she just wasn't worried about living up to his expectations. With David it was totally different. She wanted him to approve of everything she did and to see her as a good match. He was so perfect in every way that she wanted to please him and gain his admiration. It was a totally new aspect of their relationship, since they'd always been so laid-back with each other before. When they had been friends, it had never even crossed her mind to question if he liked her or not. Nevertheless, they did seem to fit perfectly...

17

It was morning, and she was again with the love of her life. Not a bad start for any day. The endorphins still raged through her system. She still felt superhuman and super happy.

With great effort, she started to think of mundane things, like what day it was, what needed to be done at the store, her schedule, and so forth. She checked her phone in bed, and found messages from Shellie, Chelsea, Kathy, and Sam. She got back to them, sending texts, calling Chelsea, and checking up on Sam.

David told her he had a meeting with his divorce lawyer later, and he intended to call Julie and ask about the baby's development. He also wanted to check again for articles about the Palazzi family in the newspapers, and he had to make some work calls and check with his team on the progress of some projects.

David prepared a delicious breakfast, and then they had some more sex just for the hell of it. They needed to test all the surfaces in the house to see if they were made for mating. She was struck by the memory of going through the same phase with Jack; they'd had sex everywhere at their home. That had been about sixteen or so years ago. She was getting older, for sure, but by all indications David didn't seem to mind.

They went their separate ways after more kissing and hugging. She couldn't wait to see him again, and felt like it would be a whole century before evening came. *How is that possible? Last month I was just a friend to him and vice versa. Now I can't live without him for half a day! Something must be malfunctioning in me. Where are all these intense feelings and emotions coming from? Again, we have to go back to the neurotransmitters…*

She started musing about biology, love, and her inability to function in a normal way. She knew all about those things that, in regular language, were called love. And she was in it, big time, head over heels. She hoped David felt the same way about her. It seemed he did, but it was just so fantastic that it scared her. *What if something bad happens? It's just not natural to be so happy...*

David was thinking about their last two days as well. He felt as if he'd finally found the woman he'd always wanted. She was fiercely loyal, gorgeous, loving, sensitive, and very social. The last was important to him, because he was that way too. He loved to be with people, had many friends, and he was sure that, with Nell, it would be easy to maintain those connections. Julie had made it difficult for him to have friends; she was jealous of both men and women. She was very pretty and vulnerable, so she had that attractive quality of a damsel in distress, but it ended there. She was a loner by nature and her friendships were very much through him. Most of his male friends' wives had tried to include Julie in their activities, but she was always a little aloof and didn't have real friends on her own. It was strange how he'd only noticed this now, and not before.

With Nell it would be totally different. She was a dream come true. She had lots of friends, threw legendary parties, and was generous to a fault. Then he remembered their romp in bed, and instantly felt a physical yearning. She was not just giving herself to the game; she was an active participant, and that was very exciting and new to him. He wanted to have her for good, so the next step was to decide how and when he should propose to her.

The fact that she was so professionally successful and independent made her even more desirable. She surely was not going to wait around for him to entertain her. He was sure they would have a very rich and exciting life together. Probably, their biggest challenge would be matching their busy schedules. Maybe it would be a great idea to go with her on her upcoming business trip to Venice, if he could clear his name by then. He could propose at the time of her store opening, which would be in a few weeks from now. He could see it now: they would sit in a gondola looking at each other on their way to dinner. He would give her a ring she would wear for the rest of her life, and she would belong to him forever...

He was softly whistling on his way to his office, so every one of his colleagues looked up as he passed. His friend Pete teasingly asked if he was okay. They'd worked together for ten years, so they knew each other pretty well. They shared a lot, discussing both their work and some of their private lives. They also went to games together, socialized, and asked each other's opinions on sensitive issues. Pete had had a girlfriend for eight years now, and David had asked him several times why he hadn't married her. He always just smiled and told him that the word "marriage" was not in his vocabulary. He loved Tess, but they didn't need a paper to prove it to anyone. David was inclined to think Tess had a different view of this issue, but he never interfered. It was their life, after all.

"I'm fine, Big Log, or should I say, I'm terrific." Pete was a big man who towered over everyone in the office at six two. But was all muscle, no mush. His girlfriend, on the other hand, was a curvaceous, petite woman with an easy laugh. David had also thought they looked a little funny together, but who's to say what love looks like? They were devoted to each other despite the "missing paper," and David was very happy to see his friend with a woman he adored.

"From the looks of it, you got lucky recently, didn't you, pretty boy?" Pete teased.

They teased each other mercilessly, and Pete considered "pretty boy" to be an annoying answer to his friend's nickname of "Big Log," so he used it a lot. David responded in kind, but then he got serious and told Pete about the new development with Nell, and that he planned to propose. He also asked if giving a ring to Nell in a gondola in Venice was a good idea.

"Oh, that's a very good idea," said Pete. "Women love romantic stuff like that. Sorry for asking, but how did the two of you get together so fast after her husband died? Was something going on between you two before?" They were good enough friends for him to ask, so David told him about his newfound attraction. Pete knew Nell and her family, and he knew of David's long friendship with her.

Pete wished his friend good luck, and as David thanked him, he privately thought he'd need it. He hadn't told anyone but Nell about the allegations in Milan, but it was a circumstance that could put the proposal on hold unless it was cleared up soon. The thought spurred him to call Franco in his office again, to see if there had been any developments. It looked like it was his lucky day. Franco's associate in Italy had just found a guest who had seen Camilla leaving the room. He'd been picking up the newspaper outside his door, and he'd looked up because she'd slammed the door with such force. He'd said she looked angry, but completely dressed, no marks of any kind and no torn clothing. Also, the polizia had found another lead, a maid who'd made a statement about letting Camilla into the room. It looked like the maid's boyfriend, a newly hired bellhop at the hotel, might have been the one to help with the slapping part. The police were about to take his statement.

David, elated by the good news, thanked Franco and asked to be kept updated. After hanging up, he ordered a case of wine to be shipped to Franco with a thank-you note and called Nell to tell her the news. She was happy to hear it, and reassured him once again that she was sure the truth would come out, and that she'd never doubted his innocence. Then they joked about innocence and the lack thereof during their nights together. After she hung up, he took care of work, then left to see another friend, who owned an upscale jewelry shop. It was time to see about that ring.

18

Nell, in the meantime, was having a very nice time with Chelsea after finishing up at the store. They happily sorted through accessories, deciding which ones Chelsea would show to Michelle for a trying-on session. They also made tea and small cucumber sandwiches, and their little mundane ceremony made them feel almost normal, almost like before the accident.

Nell needed that feeling, because although she felt completely happy around David, she didn't feel happy at home. Here, everything reminded her of Jack and their former life together, and she felt extremely guilty most of the time. She was greatly relieved about the Milan news; she hadn't doubted David, but she realized he needed to be cleared of the charges in everybody else's eyes. Otherwise, it would be impossible for him to conduct business in Italy.

She was also excited about her own upcoming trip to Venice. She loved that old, magnificent city. Despite the millions of tourists and the smell of rotten wood that permeated it, she remembered its magic, even though it had been many years since her last visit. She wished Chelsea could come too, but her daughter was in the midst of school projects and exams.

Maybe David could go with her, if he was cleared completely by then. It would be great to be with him there. It was a very romantic place, full of history and spectacular artwork, remnants of immense treasures and riches, all the trappings of power visible even today. The decay was palpable, too, but the tourists didn't care. They flocked to this dark, medieval old lady of Italy and left their money there in an ever-growing pile.

Her shop would be in a fashionable arcade close to Piazza San Marco, hopefully a little further away from the daily flood zone, but close enough for the tourists to see. She also remembered the beautiful glasses displayed in most of the shops and the tiny manufacturing places in Murano, and could not help feeling a rush of excitement.

As Nell and her daughter finished up their tea and sandwiches, Chelsea slapped her forehead. "Mom, I forgot to tell you! Your gynecologist's office left a message. They said you need to go in for a checkup soon, since you haven't been in a while. I put the number on the notepad next to the telephone. Call them back, okay?"

"Thanks, I will. Another pleasant thing on my schedule, no doubt!" They laughed, and Nell decided to give them a call the next day. She also remembered she still needed to call Shellie, but decided to wait until Chelsea was gone, since the call might include things Nell didn't feel comfortable discussing in front of her daughter, especially when it concerned a man who would be "replacing" her dad in her mother's life. It would be completely insensitive, and anyway, she didn't want Chelsea to hear about her sex life, no matter with whom. On the other hand, she would have loved the opportunity to find out about Chelsea's involvement with her boyfriend, but she didn't want to pry. Nell hoped her daughter would open up on her own, and soon, because she wanted to give her advice and be reassured about her safety. *Well, mothers of modern girls have a lot to be afraid of,* she thought.

After Chelsea left for Michelle's, Nell prepared for her evening date. She selected a light green dress with a white jacket this time, and put her green high heels on. She was happy with the result. She even put a little green eye shadow on to accentuate her catlike eyes. A few drops of her favorite spicy perfume, and she was ready to go. She was sure she'd got her outfit and makeup right, because when she stopped for cash at the bank, men took notice of her.

Two even came over to start a conversation, but she was in a hurry to see David, so politely but quickly extricated herself, and was on her way again to having a wild ride.

By this time, her anxiety had grown stronger, and she again feared that such happiness must be a sign of bad things to come. It would be unnatural to be so happy for long. On the other hand, her motto was to take life as it came, because things could always take a turn for the better. She was a fatalist, believing that she essentially had very little chance to alter the chain of events. Not because she was powerless or lacked free will, but because free will predestined certain choices on her part, despite myriad possibilities. She felt sure that, if she had to live her life again, she'd make the same decisions and mistakes, simply because of her preferences and inner compass.

To shake herself out of her contemplative mood, she called Shellie on the way over to David's. Shellie picked up at the second ring. "Hi, Nell! How's everything?"

"We're seeing each other again this evening. The sex is incredible, the guy is a dream, and he really might be in love with me. Otherwise why would he want to be with me every night? Or is it just the sex? You really think he'll propose?"

"Now, that's a little too much to answer, so slow down. I think he will—I mean, propose—and soon. As for the incredible sex, I envy you! Lucky woman! I can't wait to see what happens. This is like a live soap opera. Whatever happens, I'm on your side, but I really think he's in love with you. As for you, there are no doubts whatsoever. Even your voice changes when you speak about your knight in shining armor. He's a lucky fellow to have you, darling!"

"Thanks, Shellie! Either way, I'll keep you posted, and if he does propose, you know you need to be my bridesmaid, so do your research and prepare yourself."

"Uh-huh, heavy stuff. Will do. Anyway, enjoy your night of sin! Sorry, I meant enjoy your date!"

They laughed and hung up. Nell checked out her outfit again and noticed the paper with the gynecologist's number in her purse, so she made a mental note to herself to call them soon.

He was waiting for her, and this time he ordered in some Chinese food. He put the food on plates and served it on his glass table in the dining area. He opened a good bottle of wine and they enjoyed their evening together.

"So, tell me everything. How was your day without me?" Nell was joking, but she'd found it hard being separated from him even for a few hours. It was so good to be with him now, although she personally could not wait for the part when they would get naked. "You sent me a text about Julie having a good sonogram," she continued. "So, how is she coping? Are you more positive about the baby?"

"No and yes. The baby's fine and developing perfectly, but she's still trying to get us back together. So in that respect she's not doing okay, because I'm not reconsidering. That said, yeah, I'm getting more excited about the baby, and I want to be on good terms with her so I can be a part of my son's life. But she won't be my wife again."

"How do you know it's a boy? It could be a girl for all we know."

"I don't know; I assume since the baby is mine, it has to be a son."

"Huh! Well, aren't you the macho type! Anyway, I wasn't asking after Julie because I want you back with her, I just worry about her, with the divorce and all."

"You must be kidding me. Julie needs guidance and help even in happy times. Now she's a complete mess, she doesn't know anything except she doesn't want to be divorced. Well, too bad, I'm in love with you, so she has to find another protector for herself. Knowing her parents, they'll be babying her now and telling her what a horrible choice I was in the first place."

"David, that's cold! You seemed to be doing well before this started, and now you don't even care how she is?"

"Well, appearances can be deceiving. And just to remind you, you and Jack looked really strong too, and now look at us. Neither of us realized we liked each other more than our partners, but in reality, that *had* to be the case. Or do you think it's possible to develop these strong feelings overnight? I certainly didn't have any experience with love, but the strangest part is, now I know for sure. I recognize it. I could not and would not give up what we have now for anything or anybody. I feel like I need you to breathe normally, to be there to see my life and share it with me."

"I feel the same," said Nell softly.

"I just don't want to be away from you again," David continued. "In fact…I was wondering if it would be okay to come with you to Venice, if these charges are cleared from my name. I hope they will be. Franco seems to think it'll be any day now."

"Yes, tiger, please come with me. As for the love thing, I loved Jack, and in a way I still do, but what I feel for you is something very unique, I haven't had experience with this stuff either. Not to mention the sex. It's *so* unbelievable that sometimes I wonder if I'm dreaming."

"Speaking of sex, I was thinking about it all day long, so can we just continue our discussion of all these other things later? Come here, baby, I need you now!"

"Yes, master!"

Then they were lost to the world for a while, catching up on functional anatomy again. But this time, she wasn't worried about her performance or her imperfect body parts. She knew he loved her body the way it was. As for him, he was so absolutely sexy and well made in every respect that she couldn't have imagined a better-looking man even in her wildest fantasies. He was not overly padded, but slim and muscular, had a smooth and angular chin, a beautiful straight nose, and the best smile nature had ever created. His teeth were very white and even, and his hair was always well cut and shiny. Even his sex was perfect; it fit her in a way no previous partner's ever had.

She felt she was a pretty woman, but the kind of perfection he represented was definitely beyond her reach. It didn't seem to make a difference to him, though. His gaze held her as if she was the Venus of Milo, though she knew she didn't come even close to that sort of beauty or perfection. *Sometimes you just have to take the credit life gives you, even if it's undeserved*, she smiled to herself. She pulled him closer, eliciting an excited groan from him.

"You're incredibly beautiful, Nell. Tell me, how did I live without you?"

"I don't know, but from now on you won't be forced to. If I knew you were so sexy, I couldn't have lived without you either."

19

The next three weeks rolled by in this fashion, with everybody in differing states of anticipation. Nell wanted to go to Italy and finalize the preparations for the shop. David wanted the charges in Milan to disappear, so he could plan their trip to Venice together. Julie still anticipated David's return, though David had filed for divorce and said he was not reconsidering. Chelsea prepared for and daydreamed about the upcoming school dance, trying to take her mind off her grief over her father. Shellie was still working long hours, but trying to rebuild her life without her ex.

Sam visited Nell a few times, and the three of them had an honest discussion about the future, including the developing relationship between Nell and David. Sam had always been very close to Nell, and he recognized his dad had had a great time with her, so he was supportive. Though he believed she hadn't had an affair, he wondered privately if Nell would have been able to ignore David if his dad had lived. The outcome would have been questionable, in his opinion, but it didn't matter much now. They all loved Jack, they would all miss him, but life went on, and since Nell was young and pretty, it was natural she would end up with another man eventually. For her to pair up with someone they all knew and respected was the best possible outcome.

At the end of the second week, the phone call finally came from Franco, and David got his wish. In addition to the statements of the hotel guest, maid, and her boyfriend, a taxi driver stated that he had seen her outside of the hotel after she left the room. He said Camilla had looked fine. The polizia considered the case closed, and David was cleared of the rape charges.

As for Camilla, since her father was such an upstanding and powerful citizen, no one would even question her. In all probability, she would get away scot-free without any charges.

While David didn't want to hurt Camilla, he still wanted to clear himself in the eyes of her father and his other business associates. So David called Giuseppe.

"Pronto."

"Hi, Giuseppe, this is David Nelson. I think you know why I'm calling."

"Oh, David! Per piacere mi scusi tanto sono dispiacuto! I am so sorry, my friend. I have a good mind to disown that puttana for what she did. Please, let's not let it interrupt our business together, or our friendship…What do you say?"

"Well, I'm not sure I would really want to, but if you're serious about starting clean, I want you to notify all those business associates you warned against me," replied David. "I want you to give me your apologies in a video conference from your office with all of those people present. I also want you to ask the polizia to give you a copy of the investigation results, stating that I was cleared of all charges. I won't bring charges against your daughter, but you need to make her understand it was a very dirty and dishonest thing to do. I don't wish to be in contact with her ever again, even if we continue our business relations. If you complete these tasks, I'll consider going into business with you again."

"I will, David, and again, I apologize! I hate the fact that my own daughter made an ass out of me and caused me so much heartache. I can't trust her now. She was always very manipulative, but this is unpardonable! I'll call you with the details for the conference call and I'll FedEx you the report. I hope we can put this behind us. And do not worry, from this time on I will keep her on a very short leash. I'm very grateful to you for your understanding, and thank you! Molto grazie! Ciao!"

So David's wish was going to come true. And Nell's wish was also coming to fruition. She'd just got a call from Sofia, the local head of sales in Venice. They were all set to go for a store opening in two weeks. She called David on her cell and told him the good news, and in exchange she learned his good news. A celebration was called for, so they decided to go out for sushi and, later, champagne at the condo.

She again prepared herself for a date with her perfect man, thinking about what a lucky day it was. This time, she selected a vivid print dress and big dangling earrings with sexy high heels. When she arrived at the restaurant and noticed the stares, she was reassured that she'd chosen well. And there he was, *her* man strolling toward her and looking at her again like she was some priceless artifact instead of a middle-aged, average woman.

He certainly was a sight for sore eyes. His tight jeans gave her a good view of his powerful thighs, and his shirt, open at the neck, revealed a little of his chest. And those dreamy eyes! The man was one overwhelming "chick magnet," as Chelsea would have characterized him in teenage terminology. She wanted to just skip the whole dinner thing and go home and get naked right away, but it was too late for that. Somehow she had to endure an hour of longing, sitting so close to him that his powerful scent would invade all of her senses. It would be torture.

They went through the events and news of the day again, but she had her mind mostly on their later romp in bed. *What a predictable mind I have*, she thought. *I should be thinking about business and travel and other important issues, but I'm stuck on how nice it feels to touch his skin and be right next to him, feeling his love and desire for me.*

As for David, his excitement was also almost uncontainable. The prospect of going to Venice with Nell seemed almost sure now, and so he'd be able to propose as he wanted to, presenting the ring on a gondola ride. He wouldn't need to take the ring himself; his jeweler friend said he'd send it over to a local jewelry shop in Venice, so he could pick it up there. That certainly made it easier, especially with the tight security at airports these days.

He'd found the perfect ring for her, he was sure of it. The diamond was a large one, very bright. Somehow the solitaire and the brilliant cut just felt right. It was dominant and beautiful, just like she was. It would be a great ring for her if she accepted it. He hoped she would.

When they arrived back at the condo, they attacked each other's clothes again and threw the garments to the floor on their way to the bedroom. She could hardly wait for him to be naked so she could feast her eyes and hands on his sexy body. She pulled her dress over her head and finally pulled him over her on the bed. "Are you in the mood for some sex, lady?" He was teasing and caressing her body.

"You bet, mister. I want a big boy for dessert!"

"Your wish is my command, beautiful."

They stopped talking and got intimate, exploring all that seemed so wondrous about each other's bodies. His hands were gentle and incredibly exciting. Her own fingers explored the muscles on his back, the solid mass of his great butt—everything about him just screamed complete masculinity. She was still amazed she'd attracted this fantastic male for herself.

She was not bad looking herself, but she was sometimes almost baffled that men loved the way she looked. She was certainly not model thin, but she had big breasts and her legs were shaped very well. She knew her eyes were very good assets and she had a very friendly and open face. She also got numerous compliments on her smile, so she knew that was very attractive, but altogether, she felt far inferior compared to his physical beauty.

But David didn't seem to notice any of her shortcomings, and was taking her like she was the goddess of love. It was incredibly pleasurable. Despite all of the hardship, heartbreak, and guilt over their intimacy in the beginning, it just felt right now, and she knew she could not for the life of her ever give him up.

20

The next few days were busy. Finally the insurance company made their decision about Jack's death, ruling it an accident. That meant she would get the policy payment. It was a considerable sum, and even though she could have done without it, it would certainly help just to pay some of the taxes on the inheritance.

It was also a good thing she was now cleared of all wrongdoing, not only by the police, but by the insurance company, so she could get on with her life without the shadow of suspicion. Just the fact that David and she had started a relationship so soon after Jack's death would make some people think she'd been involved in the death somehow, but the most important aspect was what the authorities thought, and they were closing the investigation.

David received more news about Julie's pregnancy, and despite the fact that the child was not hers, Nell felt it was a very positive thing. She was afraid she wouldn't be able to give David children. She and Jack had wanted more kids after Chelsea, but she'd never been able to get pregnant. They'd decided to just accept it.

Now, if she really looked at her desires, she knew she was not very keen on another pregnancy, even if it were possible. To carry Chelsea to term had not been very easy. She'd suffered from morning sickness at the beginning, her blood pressure went up at the end, and she had pretty bad heartburn and back pain, so she was very relieved when Chelsea was born. From that minute on, it was a pleasure trip with her, but not during those first nine months.

Chelsea went to L.A. to visit Sam for the weekend, and from all the phone calls and the texts Nell got, she knew they had a great time together. She went to spend a weekend with David in Las Vegas at the same time, and they also had the time of their lives. They went to see a Cirque du Soleil show, and it was spectacular. They ate too much and made love too many times, blew a few hundred dollars on roulette and other useless, but fun, games. They went to a magic show and ate steaks, had wild sex, and went to gamble some more. Nell felt more alive, more recovered from her grief, with every passing day.

They also went shopping and bought some nice pants for David and a leather jacket with fringes for Nell. They both got over-the-top sunglasses, so when they finally put them on they looked like a couple of country singers after too many cocktails. They laughed so hard about their getups that they had to stop and gasp for breath on the sidewalk. It was a very good trip, and it showed both of them that they were compatible not only in bed, but outside of it as well.

When they got back, she went to her house and David drove back to his condo, but they agreed to have dinner together. After spending an hour away from him, she felt so alone it was horrible. Talking to Chelsea and going to the office eased her loneliness a little, but not completely. David was always at the back of her mind. She realized it how horrible it would be if things didn't work out between them. She was in love and completely taken by these feelings for him. *I doubt he'd want to marry me*, she thought. *He just got out of an unhappy marriage, and even though he loves me, I bet he'd be hesitant about getting into another long-term commitment.*

She had just bought a new iPhone with a video-conferencing feature, so she called David, who had the same model. He loved technology, so he always had the newest and best electronics available. Even in this respect they were a good match, because she just loved her gadgets. It was so nice to see him sitting behind his desk at his office and smiling at her. "I missed you, tiger."

"Hey, you. I missed you too. I can't wait for our dinner together. Where do you want to go?"

"Let's have some Italian food tonight."

"All right, we can go to Luigi's. Wear something sexy, won't you? I loved that top on you that has those dots, you know, the multicolor one. I mean, sorry for the special request, I was just remembering our time together. It was incredible! You know I love you, baby."

"I love you too. I'm not sure where that top is, it could be at the cleaner's. But even if I can't find that one, I'll wear something that catches your eye, how about that?"

"Sounds like a plan!"

"Ciao, handsome, see you in a few hours!"

"I can't wait!"

As she hung up, Nell missed him already. So she busied herself with things she needed to do for the office and reviewing the plans for the store in Venice. It seemed that her life was on track again. Despite Jack falling out of her life, she still had the kids and a fantastic man who seemed to love and care for her a great deal. The question was, of course, how much. Was it something for keeps, or only a temporary relief for them after a stressful time in their lives? She was certainly hoping for the first option. She could not imagine anything more exciting or pleasurable than marrying Mr. Perfect.

The top was at the cleaner's, so she decided on a miniskirt and a spaghetti-strap top she thought David would consider sexy. It had a built-in bra, so her boobs sat a little lower than in her regular bras, but it still looked good in her opinion. The one thing that bothered her was that if the evening got a little colder, her nipples might show through the thin fabric. Although David might find that a bonus, she didn't like the thought, so she picked up a short-sleeved silk jacket as well. Another pair of high heels and a smart purse, a little eye makeup, and just a touch of bronzer, and she was ready to go.

As soon as she opened the door, David pulled her into his embrace and started to kiss her passionately, only stopping to nibble on her earlobe and whisper, "I think you look even better in this one, lovely lady! Can we just order something in later? You look good enough to eat..."

"Come on, you wanted me to put on this top only so I could take it off? Let's go to dinner and come back later. We'll have the whole night. I'm hungry."

In response, he trailed little kisses down her neck and to her breast. Her top was already halfway to the floor, and she was grabbing for his bottom to hold onto somehow. The man was an animal, but how lucky was that! She'd never before had this overwhelming desire for any man, blinding and more urgent than anything she could imagine. By now she was halfway gone. She thought after another half a minute she'd come. He pulled her panties to the side, pulled her legs up around his waist, and they had the hottest sex right then and there in the foyer, leaning on the wall, almost fully clothed. Just as she thought, she was coming by the time he entered her, and then he pleasured her with another earth-shattering orgasm by the time his release came.

Her first coherent thought after her legs slid back to the ground was, *How come I never knew such fantastic sex was possible? How come I assumed what I had with Jack was normal?* If that had been normal, this was stratospheric. Not only had they had sex far more often then she'd ever experienced with Jack, but it was so satisfying that it was hard to put into words. She'd never known she was capable of such wild and barbaric behavior— because she was sure this was not the kind of sex any civilized society would label as normal or okay. *So* wild and out of control, and so absolutely fucking good (no pun intended), there were no terms to describe it.

I'd better cancel those therapy sessions I started after Jack's death! I would not and could not speak about my sex life with anyone! Imagine giving a description of some of the things I did with David, she thought.

What was so surprising was how different sex could be with different men. With Jack it was more about love and connection, and it always felt relaxing and lovely. With David it was varied each time, but always horrendously exciting and more pleasurable than anything else. It felt urgent and shamefully wild, something she wouldn't want anyone to know about, not even her best friends. It wasn't relaxing; it was mind-blowing. It wasn't about love and connection; it was about possessing someone completely and without any limits. They took each other as if they were drinking a glass to the last drop, never leaving anything at the bottom. When David took her, she felt molten for that short time, not as a separate person, but rather living in an altered world in which the two of them mixed together for a while. It was exhilarating and shameful, beautiful and scary, all at the same time.

Almost as if answering her musings, David nudged her shoulder and asked, "So was it worth not going out, lovely lady? Do you feel like some more exercise for the night?"

"Hey, anytime, Mr. Perfect. Although I don't understand why I never get tired of having sex with you. You must have some magic."

"Yeah, I have a magic wand, and I'm not afraid to use it." He was teasing, and his eyes were laughing at her. "You want to borrow my magic wand for a little bit, babe?"

"Sure, why not? You think I envy you, don't you—that you have one and I don't?"

"Listen to you, Ms. Doctor. Penis envy? Come on, that's such an old fable, you of all people should know better."

"Ah, then why were you so sure your offspring would be a boy? Face it, it's still a man's world out there. But I don't mind, as long as I get the only perfect male left on our planet."

"Now that sounds better! As for it being a man's world out there, I don't see you hurting or suffering because of your gender, do I? But we've had enough talk. Why don't you just concentrate on the pleasures of life for a while?"

This was probably how an addiction felt. She just could not get enough of him and his body. The more she got, the more she wanted. So they had sex in three other positions before even realizing that they were hungry. Finally they ended up eating sandwiches from his refrigerator and continued their sex sessions afterward. It was totally worth skipping dinner, in her opinion.

By the morning she was spent and happy again. Despite the temptation to lounge around, she picked herself up, went home to change clothes, then went to the store to work. David left for the office and said he would call later. She suggested they wait to see each other until the following day, because she felt she needed to spend a night home with Chelsea. They agreed, but it wasn't as easy as she thought it would be. Though they talked on the phone and texted each other almost every hour, she felt a physical yearning to be close to him, to see and touch him, and missed him constantly.

This was getting insane, but felt good anyway.

21

Finally they were in Venice. They stayed in a small room in Hotel Flora close to Piazza San Marco. Despite being in an alleyway, the room was intimate and charming, with a huge bed and its own bathroom. They had access to a little garden, a small oasis in the built-in quarter.

Only minutes away were the piazza, the Grand Canal, and little cafes and restaurants. The characteristic small bridges crossing over smaller waterways looked like the backs of fighting cats, arching up in the middle. The gondolas were everywhere, and the Vaporetto station and Doge's Palace were next door. The row of little shops where her new place would be opening was close as well. It was an ideal setting for both business and romance.

They had already gone to see the horse statues on the roof of the basilica, seen the view from the top of the Campanile, walked on the Rialto Bridge, and eaten some excellent gelato on the way. Venice was an experience not to be missed.

But she had work to do too. Sofia turned out to be a friendly middle-aged woman with a severe bun on the top of her head and silver-framed spectacles. She welcomed Nell like a family member, and introduced her associates, two younger ladies who would be the salespeople. They both were pleasant, and Nell was sure they would work out just fine.

Then Nell excitedly examined the stock. The layout for the store was already there, but the racks were still missing and some of the shelves had their places marked but were not on the wall yet. The wallpaper had a very interesting pattern, and though Nell was not sure if it was a good idea in such a humid area, Sofia assured her she had the same kind of wall covering at home, and it never got moldy. She had lived all her life in Venice, so Nell trusted her opinion.

Nell decided to decorate the shop windows with a few glass pieces and traditional venetian masks. She planned to hang up a chandelier at the top of the window, on whose arms she'd place elegantly dressed mannequins. Flanking the window would be two mannequins in masks and some beautiful vases. In the background, she wanted to display scarves and fabrics that would unite the scene. She did not like standard-issue mannequins; hers were especially detailed and lifelike, made by an Italian company.

The printed materials and other ad items were top quality, since David's company had made them. His designs were always successful, so she was sure they would help her sales get started. They also decided to display enlarged photos of Nell's other stores on the wall between the shelves and the racks of garments. All in all, she was very satisfied and was sure they would have a great start.

David and Nell took Sofia out for dinner that night, and learned many interesting facts about Venice and its history. Sofia invited them to her place the next week, so it seemed she was taken with her American boss and her companion. They worked hard all week to put everything into place for the opening next Saturday, because Nell wanted to have some time left for last-minute touches or changes.

On Friday evening after dinner, David suggested they go on a gondola ride on Saturday. Nell thought it was a fine idea. They hadn't had much time for each other, except during the nights, of course, which were steamy and fantastic. She thought David seemed to enjoy her more and more. She'd asked him if he was sick of being with her constantly, but he assured her that it was what he wanted. They did not have many friends here anyway, but they both kept up with their families and friends through e-mail, calls, and texting. They both seemed to be walking on clouds.

She was not sure what to wear for the evening outing in the gondola, but finally decided she would wear a longer summer dress with a bolero. The fabric was black with large yellow dots. The hem of the dress and the bolero were edged with yellow. At the last minute she grabbed a black cat mask, and she thought it looked great. David looked sexy as always in simple gray slacks, a corn-yellow shirt, and a dark brown suede jacket.

She had the usual butterflies in her stomach, since he was sitting so close that their thighs were touching. She wondered how long this feeling of unreal excitement would last—a year or two, or just for a few months? She hoped it would be for the rest of their lives. By now she felt David shared her strong feelings, so in her head they would be together forever...whatever that meant in human terms.

David put his arms around her shoulder and told her how sexy she looked, so again she felt immersed and happy. The gondolier, a nice young man in a striped polo and a straw hat, was quiet and avoided looking at them. Usually gondoliers told facts and stories about the scenes they were seeing on the way, but not this time. Nell had the suspicion that was at David's request, because he'd exchanged an almost conspiratorial glance with the gondolier as they got in. Before she had more time to wonder what David was planning, he pulled out a black velvet box from his pocket and placed it very gently into her palm.

"Open it, my love. I really hope it's to your liking." Nell opened the box with shaking hands and found a very beautiful and quite large solitaire ring inside. It was shining brightly, and she absolutely loved it on sight.

"We might have to wait a little, but I want to marry you. Will you accept?" David asked her.

"Are you sure about this? Because if you are, I think I will!"

"I'm more sure of it than anything else. I want to be with you for the rest of my life. Will you marry me, Nell?"

"Yes, I will!"

With that he put the ring on her finger. It fit her perfectly. She felt it suited her perfectly as well; the stone might be a little large, but with diamonds, they say the bigger the better. It was gorgeous beyond description. As for the man who gave it to her, there was no description either. She was completely swept from reality and all other concerns in her life and was again melting into this man, who, as far as she was concerned, could have been the living version of Michelangelo's David. He was unbelievably sexy and caring, and he was offering her much happiness to come. After the accident and the funeral, it was a promise of a new, beautiful future.

The gondola put them down close to their hotel, and it was time to go somewhere private, because David was devouring her like she was a very appetizing meal. It wasn't a scene fit for public display. He gave the gondolier a pretty large sum of money, as far as Nell could see, then practically pulled her at a run straight to their hotel room.

Then they were on the bed, wrestling to remove their last undergarments. David told her that he wanted to see her wearing only the ring. She felt a little too exposed; she was always concerned about her weak areas. Again David took the uncertainties away, caressing her, whispering encouragements in her ear, and looking at her in a way that made her feel truly beautiful.

Nell, surprised and happy, was tingling all over from his ministrations. She couldn't believe her luck. She'd had a good man in her life, but to end up the second time with the perfect man... She was the luckiest woman on earth. Shellie had been right; she'd predicted that he would propose in a month, and he had.

She didn't have much time to think, though, because the sensations he sparked in her pushed away anything cerebral or remotely intelligent. This time he was very slowly making love to her, taking his time and making her cry out with pleasure all the way. His hands traveled up on her spine, his erection pushed against her abdomen, until finally she let him get in to push her to higher levels of pleasures. All the time, he whispered into her ear and let his tongue travel all the way to her nipple and back to her mouth, kissing her, looking into her eyes as she came in big, shiny waves of rapture. He came right after she felt her climax slowing. In that moment, it seemed like a good enough reason to live: to love and be loved the way they just had.

Her fleeting thought was, *It's a pity human sex isn't a longer act. It would've been nice to spend more time in such a high.* Luckily, David felt the same way she did, because they repeated the act a few more times before morning came. Some sessions were fast and furious, some slow and languid, but all of them made their bond stronger and more solid. As always, the level of intimacy was amazing. She always had the urge to touch and explore all of his body, but somehow it was so beautiful and humbling that he seemed to have the same desire about *her* body. One of the reasons she'd chosen to study medicine was because of her admiration for the human body, but this was on another level entirely.

One time, between their sex sessions, he asked her what she was thinking.

"Well, I was thinking about you and me and our future marriage and the universe…"

"The universe?"

"Yeah. How is it that physics and forces so clean and sterile they could mathematically describe our universe produce something so utterly weird as brains? Why would stars produce planets with living organisms that have feelings and consciousness? And why do these organisms have orgasms? How on earth can you fit feelings and stuff that couldn't be described by anything mathematical or physical into the unfeeling, unknowing system of stars and planets and gravitational forces and supernovas..."

"Wow, maybe you need more sex to solve all those riddles, babe, because my brain sure doesn't have answers for your questions. They're very interesting, though. If I didn't know better, I'd think you were taking drugs."

"I did take a drug, tiger. It's called "David," and I love the effect, so I'm going to take it again."

"Fine by me, my little speck of stardust."

"Tease all you want, but I still don't get it. Maybe the only reason is that old saying, 'because it could.'"

"Because it could what?"

"Oh, you know, if someone asks you why you did some crazy or unbelievable thing, you can say, 'Because I could.' That's what I meant here. Maybe there's no reason, it's only our brains searching for it."

"Well, babe, my brain isn't as active as my other body parts, so can we pause the philosophy for now? I'd rather study physiology, not astronomy!"

"Okay, okay, but I want to ask you one more thing. Why do you want to marry me? Are you sure about this? I remember how many girlfriends you had before Julie. Why would you want to stay with me when you're free again?"

"That's an easy question, Nell. Because I love you. I truly do. The test for that is to imagine being without you. And when I do, I feel terrible, I miss you too much. I feel I can't live without you at my side. I was hoping you felt the same way. Don't you?"

"Of course I do! Love you, I mean. And I feel the same way. I don't want to be without you. I was just asking because it's a little different for women, or at least I think it is."

"Then we're in agreement about everything. And as for the differences between men and women, I'd rather show you than talk about it, love." David rolled on top of her.

"Just one more question," Nell resisted. "When did you first know you loved me?"

"I had no idea I had these feelings for you until our kiss at my condo. That was when I felt for sure that we belonged together. As for when I realized I wanted to spend the rest of my life with you, it was the ball. I knew I had to have you for sure, and I'd do anything in my power to achieve my goal. Now, can we finally be physical instead of verbal for a while? You can tell me everything later, I promise."

"I think you're lying."

"I think you might be right, my lady of the universe..."

Afterward, she felt so relaxed and happy she didn't feel like talking again, not even about the vastness of the universe. As far as she was concerned, David was her universe, and what a universe it was!

She felt now that they truly belonged to each other. By the time she drifted to sleep, she was not sure if she would ever feel "normal" again—nor did she want to.

22

They returned to the States two weeks after the opening of the store and after more memorable times in gorgeous Venice. They decided to hold the wedding in six months. Partly because of bad memories, they planned to have it in Hawaii instead of California. Nell thought a small, intimate affair would be lovely, and David agreed.

Everyone was happy for them, including Jack's friends. No one seemed to fault them for their newfound love and happiness; they were radiating such bliss it was obviously the right state for them to be in. Even Sam seemed okay with the fact that his stepmom had found love so fast after his dad's death, and he congratulated them. Chelsea was also supportive, still sad from time to time, but approving of their marriage plans. Shellie was gloating, and told Nell several times what a good judge of character she was—except when it came to selecting her own husbands. They laughed, had dinner together, and Nell told her about the experience and the proposal.

The only unhappy person from their old life seemed to be Julie. She was angry about the divorce and very abusive in terms of giving her opinion about the match, but she had an excuse: the pregnancy. There hadn't been any problems so far; David had seen the sonograms and was impressed by the little fetus and its development. Nell didn't see the pictures, but David told her about them. She thought it was a blessing to have the baby, and she was again relieved that she wouldn't be responsible for that part of David's future. She would have loved to carry his child, but feared it at the same time. And given her age, it might not be a simple undertaking. This way, David's "immortality" was assured, and they had a pressure-free relationship ahead of them.

⌒

She was in a bridal boutique looking at dresses when the call came from David. Julie had started bleeding and was sent to the hospital. He was going to visit her and see if everything was okay. Nell was worried, but by that evening Julie was sent home and given medication. According the doctors, she had only a slight chance of losing the pregnancy. That didn't make her calm, though. Julie was hysterical and frightened, and required both of her parents' skill just to keep from crying. When David came home to the condo, he looked tired and sad.

"Hi, love. How are things going?" asked Nell, giving him a hug.

"Not very well, I'm afraid. You know Julie. She was always very dramatic, and now she has a reason to be, so it's pretty bad. I'm not sure the doctor is right, telling her it's going to be okay. Although it's just a statistical analysis, you can't really tell. Julie's parents are worn out, and she's hysterical. I hope it'll be fine."

"Let's hope it will be! Do you want to drink something?"

"Normally I wouldn't, but I think I'll make an exception tonight. Give me a martini, beautiful."

"Coming right up. Did they tell her when to go back for another checkup?"

"Yes, I think in a week or so. I'll call tomorrow and ask how everything is, but I don't want to visit her at home. If she goes in for another sonogram I might wait for her there at the hospital, but I want to disengage from her as much as possible. I'll spend time with the baby, but I don't wish to spend more time with

Julie than absolutely necessary. Now I can't even remember why I married her."

"Well, I hope you won't be saying the same things about our marriage in a few years."

"Never. I could never forget why I married you, baby. If for nothing else, the loan from buying that bling will remind me."

"Oh, so you'll stay married to me to pay back the ring? That's nice! You also want me to buy you a new sports car every year or what?"

"Hey, I have some other reasons, too. If you come here, I can show them to you."

"Don't always go there! Everything's about sex with you. I want to believe that you love my brain the most."

"Of course I do. Right after I have your other parts, baby, I'll absolutely worship your brain, too. You are one of those rare women with both the looks and the brains. I'm a lucky man indeed!"

And there they were again, coupling like rabbits in springtime, paying no heed to the warnings from fate that all might not be well for long.

Julie lost the baby four days after that. She was devastated, angry, and made David's life as miserable as she could. He was sad and sorry, but the extra blame and unpleasantness made it worse. Nell tried to ease his pain and sadness as much as she could, and even offered to postpone the wedding for a few months, but David didn't want to hear about it. He said it was life; not everything worked out as expected.

Julie's parents took her somewhere in the Midwest to visit some relatives, and so everything got more quiet. The feelings of loss and sadness still lingered, though, and Nell wished it could have been different.

In the meantime, she'd found the reminder about her gynecological checkup, so she made an appointment at the office. Now that David didn't have his own child, it might be important to find out if she could give him one. She wasn't a big stickler for physicals; she never felt sick, so she hadn't had a checkup of any kind for a few years. She hoped she'd get a clean bill of health.

The evening before the checkup, she and David stayed at the condo and barbecued a filet mignon. It was delicious. They were cleaning the table and putting the dishes into the dishwasher, when David said, out of the blue, "I was already thinking of the baby's eye color, believe it or not. I was wondering if he or she would have the straight nose everyone on my dad's side has, at least the men."

Nell could tell from the way his shoulders sagged that he was really grieving the little baby he'd lost. She put the plate in the dishwasher, but was unable to say anything in response as she realized how much this child must have meant to him. She put her hand on his shoulder and felt him relax. He let her turn him around and kiss him. This time it was more for comfort than for anything else, but she wanted to give it to him, no matter what. He was a kind man, and an awful thing had just happened to him.

In that moment, her feelings about children changed. She'd had a difficult first pregnancy, but who knew? Even that might be better with this man. He was such a blessing it was unbelievable. She wanted to give him a blessing in return.

Later, in bed, she told him that if he agreed, they could try for a baby. "I'm sure your kid would be good-looking and smart as a whip," she said. "And also tough to handle, just like you!"

David laughed. "I have no idea what I was like as a kid, but we can ask Aunt Sally or Uncle Jim." David's parents had died in a traffic accident when he was fifteen. He still had fond memories of them, but he was raised for the rest of his childhood in his aunt and uncle's house. He still went to visit them regularly, and had several nieces and nephews in the area. The aunt and uncle were a lovely couple, Nell remembered.

"I bet you were also a difficult child," David teased. Nell smiled but didn't answer, thinking about her own childhood. She was also an only child. Her father had died of a heart attack when she was three, so she didn't remember him except for the pictures her mother had showed her later. Her mom had died of a stroke when Nell was twenty. It had been a very traumatic time for her, but she was already close to David at the time, and he'd helped her through her grief. To this day she tried to eat well and stay fit to avoid an early death like her parents. Thinking about it made her realize that she probably needed to check her arteries and cholesterol. *Maybe they can do a blood panel at the gynecologist's office*, she thought.

"So do you want us to try, tiger? I mean for the little baby," she asked.

"Sure, if you don't mind. I think you'd look incredibly sexy as a pregnant woman, and if our kid had your looks and my drive, I wouldn't have to complain about anything. As a matter of fact, we can even try for it now! What do you say?"

"That you are incorrigible, and I love you for it."

Sex...she had to admit it was a very pleasant activity. But pregnancy was scary. Men had it easy, but what was new about that? They always got the easier side, she mused.

But children were worth it. Just thinking about Chelsea made her happy. Everyone deserved the chance to feel that special connection that nobody but your own child could offer. It was different from the bond with your parents or with your spouse; it was overpowering, it overrode all other things in importance.

She thought it would be a lovely thing for David to feel that way about his own offspring. She felt producing an heir was a very important thing for any human, and despite the fact that she understood people who did not wish to have children, she thought they were missing out big time. It was saddening to think of all those previous generations losing their chance to capture a tiny part of the future. Although, again, what would it mean to them? Since they were gone forever, not much. Still, she thought bringing children into the world was a purpose worthy of all the effort, strength, and dedication she had.

23

As usual, she was a little nervous about her appointment. She was wearing a flowery summer dress and strappy sandals, so her gynecologist commented on her nice outfit. He was a nice guy, sexy and stylish, and he loved to flirt with her. But his real value was that he was one of the best specialists in San Diego. He said on the whole everything looked normal, but he ordered a list of tests, a blood panel, some hormone tests, and even a lipid panel to see where she was. He asked her to come back in a week to discuss the results of the blood test. She mentioned her intention of getting pregnant again, since she was remarrying and her future husband did not yet have a biological child. The doctor, who knew David socially, congratulated her, and recommended that David get checked out as well. They parted smiling, and she felt elated just thinking about the possibilities of a little life that would be hers and David's.

After the appointment, she had lunch with Chelsea. They ate excellent veggie burgers with salad, and chatted about Chelsea's studies and their next few months. Chelsea asked if she could spend some time at the office and learn more about Nell's shops in general. Nell was pleased; she thought it would be a great idea for Chelsea to see how her business worked. Maybe she would become interested in it, if she had any time left over after all her schoolwork. She was very bright, so studying was not hard for her at all.

After a very pleasant time, Chelsea left to go back to their house, and Nell went back to David's condo to spend the night there. Before David got home, she called Shellie and caught up with some other friends. Then David arrived, and they took a shower together and ate sandwiches in front of the TV. Some action movie was on, but they missed half of it on account of smooching and other hanky-panky. *Ah well*, Nell thought, *this type of action is much more interesting than movie action.*

By now, she'd stored several outfits at David's condo so she wouldn't always have to make an extra trip to get fresh clothes, and so she would feel more home at his place. He was very supportive, helping her pick out what to bring and cleaning out a section of his walk-in closet. Nell noticed that all of David's choices were her more provocative, sexy pieces. He loved to see her in an outfit that screamed for attention. Not that she minded. She had tons of outfits, but most would fit into this category. She liked to show off her legs and her curves.

In short, she loved to be a woman and enjoyed male attention, flirting, and cultivating male friends. Some of those male friends would have probably loved to have a shot at something more, but were content just to hang around and enjoy her personality rather than her sexuality. As for her, she'd never cheated on Jack, though she'd had numerous offers, some crude, some harder to refuse. It had been worth it to be faithful, because she'd recognized Jack's dedication and genuine love, and because she was sure he also hadn't stepped outside of their marriage—even though he could have, big time. He was very popular with women: patients, nurses, and even some of his colleagues had idolized him. David, too, was popular, but she felt completely confident in him.

The next few days were spent with office work and organization and in gathering news from the Venice store and from the others abroad. They all seemed to be in good shape. Kathy, her assistant, showed her a great new computer system that balanced the sheets daily to their actual value. Kathy also had some of the old office furniture replaced, and the workplace looked more hip and modern. They also enjoyed Chelsea's input. She showed up and had some fresh ideas of where to order new and interesting items. It seemed she had a good eye for the constant changes and development that are part of every business.

Whenever Nell was away, it was Kathy who took the helm. She had done a great job, so Nell decided to give her a larger bonus at the next term. Kathy was also loyal to a fault. Nell remembered once, when her cell phone had lost its reception, Jack had called the office to find out Nell's whereabouts. Kathy had refused to tell him, because Nell had left instructions saying she didn't want to be bothered by anyone. Kathy took it literally, and Jack hadn't been able to get a hold of Nell until she returned later that day. They still laughed about that sometimes. Luckily, Jack hadn't been offended; instead, he'd thought it was a good thing that Kathy was so protective of her boss. Nell appreciated her loyalty as well, and so she'd given her more and more responsibilities. So far, she hadn't been disappointed in Kathy's performance or attitude.

Nell's store inventory reflected her own personal tastes. She loved clothes that were sexual and dramatic, but on the elegant side. She disliked and refused to sell too-flashy or low-cut dresses. She was a big believer in fitted clothing, so she referred her customers to her tailor, who always fixed anything that did not fit like a glove. She also had a penchant for jewelry, and in addition to selling it, she owned literally hundreds of earrings, bracelets, and necklaces, from valuable gems to worthless stuff she'd bought for pennies. In the store, she created mixed displays of merchandise, pairing dresses with jewelry and scarves of the same hues and organizing her shelves by color. She also loved large photographs of gorgeous places, animals, and cars, anything that piqued her interest. She'd read somewhere that landscapes and animal pictures made people happy, and that was what she was aiming for in her store. Her talent lay in creating arrangements that accentuated and flattered the individual elements. Looking at her financial numbers, it seemed she'd hit the nail right on the head. And the best part was that she had so much fun in the process. She just adored fashion: the shoes, the fur, the rings, all of it.

She was at David's condo, folding tops and putting them on a shelf, when David finally came in and embraced her from behind. As usual, she responded to his touch with a small tremor in her belly. He made her nervous in a good way, all that anticipation and excitement making her cheeks flushed and her voice husky. She was normally so cool under pressure, but when David came close, she collapsed on herself like warm chocolate. She even felt the oozing and sweetness coming out of her pores; she was ready to be consumed more than anything, again and again and again…

"Why don't you model some of these clothes for me, baby?" he whispered into her ear, biting it very gently. Nell felt a shiver running up and down her spine. The feeling was exquisite. Then came the licking, adding another layer of pleasure and fueling her readiness to be taken. She was wearing her dress from the office, since she hadn't changed yet. He was already pulling it above her head and pushing himself into her back, so instead of the cool fabric, now she felt his thighs and chest burning her from behind. Even with pants and shirts on, he felt hot and solid, hard and sexy. He was taking those pants off. He pointed to a short cocktail dress hanging between more formal dresses. It was of a thin, peacock-blue satin. "I want you to put it on. No bra or panties, please."

He smiled wickedly at her shocked expression and continued his undressing. She not only felt him, but saw him in the mirror facing her. She got into the dress, feeling pretty self-conscious, but he didn't seem to mind.

"But look, my breasts are flattened in it. And my nipples will make holes in this dress!" she joked.

"That's exactly the effect I want, love. I want to see your nipples through the fabric. Now I'll free them from the dress. How about that?" He did just that, pulling down the top part of the dress to expose her breasts.

"I always knew you were a gentleman, tiger."

"As for the panties, I don't miss them at all. Do you?"

"No, I don't miss them...but we never got to the modeling part..."

"I think this part is even more interesting, don't you agree, darling?"

"Hmm, yes. I'll do whatever you tell me, tiger..."

He pulled the dress up and set her on top of the built-in commode, so her bottom was halfway supported, and pushed himself inside her. "Ah, so nice! You're always ready for me, aren't you, baby? I love that about you."

"I think I can say the same about you. Are you always so horny, or is this only for me?"

"That's a trade secret, darling, but can we have more action and less talk now?"

"Aye, aye, sir!" she whispered into his ear, letting her tongue explore.

"Make sure never to wear this dress to a party if you don't want me to embarrass myself and you, love," David mumbled.

She was sure to remember this dress for the rest of her days, she thought, before he took everything out of her mind again. "I'll keep it forever to reminder us of how naughty and wicked we are," she whispered.

He was going faster and more furiously than ever, and she felt herself letting go. Her last coherent thought was about babies, before the waves of pleasure closed over her head. He made her off-the-charts happy, and she wanted to give back somehow. It would be very beautiful to make a life now and give him the news as a present...

24

She went back to the gynecologist's office the next Monday. The doctor came in promptly and seemed to be in a very somber mood. He greeted her with a half smile, sat down, and spoke directly. "Nell, I have some bad news for you. Don't fret, it's not anything life threatening, but you won't like it. I don't think you're going to have another baby. I'm terribly sorry. You're healthy otherwise, but your fertility is gone at this point. It's not completely impossible, but your chances are so low that I'd be selling dreams if I told you that you'd be successful in getting pregnant."

Nell was so shocked that she couldn't say a word. She just stared at the doctor while crumbling to pieces inside. It couldn't be true! But he was a specialist, so he surely was telling her the facts.

Seeing her shock, he came over to her side, put his hand on her shoulder, and continued gently, "You see, you had an infection some time ago. Most likely you didn't notice it at all, but your tubes are gone. They're full of scar tissue. And from the hormone checkup, your ovaries don't seem to be producing usable eggs anymore. I'm really sorry to tell you this."

"But I feel fine! I had no symptoms, and I didn't notice any signs of my hormones being gone," she mumbled, trying to make sense of the bad news.

"They aren't gone, just very low, so it's hard to notice. It's just your fertility and your ability to get pregnant that have changed. I have to be honest with you, I really think your chances are almost nil. It's not impossible, you probably have a 0.1 to 0.5 percent chance, but that's very low."

"Can it be surgically or hormonally fixed?"

"I'm afraid not. They've tried it before, but the results weren't good at all. It's entirely up to mother nature if she wants to give you a miracle or not. I can give you a low-dose hormone replacement, but the effects are questionable. It might not hurt, but most likely it won't help either."

After a sad shake of his head, he continued, "At least your lipid panel is perfect, so you're very healthy otherwise. Again, I didn't tell you getting pregnant was impossible, but it's definitely not a likely scenario."

"Well, thank you, Doctor. Thanks for being honest and straightforward. It's better to know than to hope for something that won't happen. If you don't think the hormones would help much, I'd prefer not to take them."

"All right then. I'll just schedule a mammogram for you in six months. And please come back for another checkup in a year."

He shook her hand and let her go, as if what had transpired were perfectly normal.

She was devastated. She thought she wouldn't reach her car. Somehow, driving on autopilot, she got home and closed herself in her room for a while. She wanted to scream, but that wouldn't help anyway.

After staring into space for a half hour, she got up and got a suitcase from the garage. She took it to her closet and packed it with things she could use on a trip. Mostly summer things, dresses, jackets and shorts. She needed to get away.

She sent a text to Shellie, then called Kathy to see if she had some time to see her. Kathy was home and happy to see what Nell wanted. Nell drove over and explained that she was leaving, and that she needed Kathy to hold the fort while she was away.

Kathy was supportive, though she tried to talk Nell out of her plan of leaving. But when she realized how seriously Nell wanted to go, she promised to help. She took notes about the business, and when that was done, she let Nell talk to the airlines and her friends in privacy. Hours later, Nell came to Kathy in the kitchen and told her she was set to go. She told her she wanted to stay abroad for at least six months, and didn't want anyone to know where she went. She made Kathy promise to shield Nell from anyone who tried to stop her, and to be her liaison for the family. Nell would take a new cell phone, and leave her beloved iPhone with Kathy.

"Is David the reason you're going away? Did he do something awful or unforgivable to you?" asked Kathy.

"No, don't think that. He's a fantastic man, and I love him dearly, but I can't marry him. I can't tell you my reasons, but believe me, they're good ones. I just need to give him the chance to find someone else."

"But why? He's totally in love with you!"

"I can't explain, but trust me on this, Kathy. If he married me now, he'd regret it later, so I have to give him back his freedom. I don't want him to track me down and come after me either. Please, Kathy, you have to promise not to tell him anything."

"Well, I wouldn't, you know that. I don't actually even know where you're headed, anyway. What should I tell Chelsea? She's going to be frantic! How can you leave her behind?"

"I'll call often, and we'll talk. I think she's ready. She's a young adult, and she needs to try her wings without me. You can take care of her and my shop, so everything will be fine. Look at this as the extended vacation you've wanted me to take for years."

"But I didn't mean it like this! David will be devastated. He'll search for you whether you want him to or not, I don't doubt it. As for Chelsea being ready, I'm not so sure. She'll miss you, especially after Jack's death."

"Oh, Kathy, please don't make it harder for me. You know I love you, and I love Chelsea, and I'm absolutely in love with David. That is why I can't marry him. Trust me on this!" Nell was near tears.

"I wish I could, but I have this sinking feeling you're convincing me to let you make the biggest mistake of your life. Are you *sure* this is the right way of dealing with whatever is bothering you? Is this about some major health issue you're not telling anyone about?"

"I'm not dying or mortally sick, so don't worry about my health. I just have to go and be away for a while. Whether it's a mistake or not, I have no choice. Either way I need to do this, and I need you to keep my whereabouts a secret. I'll call you, so I'm sure you'll figure it out soon enough, but keep it to yourself, Kathy, please!"

"All right, you know I'm loyal to you. I just wish you would do something I could approve of or understand."

"Hey, you're not the only one with that wish. See you in a few months, my friend!"

They hugged each other, and Nell hopped in a cab headed for the airport. Kathy had promised to take Nell's Cobra home the next day. She watched Nell's cab drive away as long as the brake lights were visible. *She has some hard times ahead of her,* Kathy thought, and felt sorry that her true friend was running away. *It must be one hell of a problem that's scaring her away, because she's never been a quitter.* Kathy assumed it had to be somehow a moral issue or misguided guilt that was driving Nell away. What a waste for such a beautiful love story to end this way. She was sure she'd never seen happier lovers than Nell and David.

~

A few hours later, all hell broke loose. Chelsea wanted to know where Nell had gone, and David came to Kathy's house demanding information that she could not and would not give. She handed him the letter Nell had left for him, and watched his face become pale and set as he read it.

"*My dearest David,*

I am sorry to leave you, I really am. I do love you with all my heart, but I still can't go through with this marriage. Please, take the ring back. I gave it to Kathy. Look for someone more suited to you to fall in love with. We're not a good match, I'm afraid.

I will be going away. Please let me be and don't come after me. I will stay away for six months or longer, I don't know. I will contact everyone in my family and Kathy will be my messenger, but let her be, too. She doesn't know where I am.

You might hate me after this or still keep loving me, I don't know, but I will always love you, David, forever!

Nell"

David was devastated. He had no idea what could have caused Nell to run out on him like this. They'd been so happy even yesterday, so something must have happened in the last twenty-four hours. He decided to find out everything Nell had done after they'd last seen each other, and told Kathy to let him know as soon as Nell called. "Please, you realize I can't *not* search for her!" he exclaimed. "I love her and want to marry her, and whatever changed her mind about our future marriage, I need to convince her otherwise. I understand you promised to keep her secret, but please at least let me know she's safe somewhere when she surfaces, okay?"

"Will do, David. And just so you know, I tried to change her mind about this. I think she should have stayed and tried to solve whatever it is she's worried about here, with you. I also worry about Chelsea. She's going to take it hard, being abandoned like this. But Nell was so set on going, I couldn't convince her to stay."

"I know, Kathy. I know you want the best for her. That's why I'm asking you this time to consider overruling her request and helping me find her. I won't push you more, but I want you to know that whatever it is, I want to fix it and be her lifelong companion. I love her more than anything."

"I believe you, David, and I promise to help you as much as my loyalty lets me. I'll call you and Chelsea as soon as I hear from her."

David went straight to call Franco, giving him all the available information and asking him to search for Nell's location immediately. Franco said Nell might be easier to find than she thought, since she had to use her passport to go to Europe. She must be traveling under her married name or her maiden name; there were not many other possibilities. He thought Italy or Hungary could be possible destinations, since she had two stores in Italy already and one in Budapest. Amsterdam and Paris might be also possible destinations, or perhaps she had gone to London. Franco promised David a fast answer.

In the meantime, Kathy was consoling a distraught Chelsea, serving her tea and explaining that her mom seemed worried about something but otherwise healthy. Chelsea also had a letter from Nell.

"My lovely Chelsea,

I hope you won't hate me for abandoning you for a while. I needed to get away for a few months, I just couldn't go through with the marriage. He did nothing wrong, I want you to know that, and I'm okay, I don't have a disease that's killing me, so don't worry. I know that you will feel lonely for a while, but we will communicate through Kathy. I'm sure you will help at the office, and that you will do fantastically in your studies. You are the best daughter ever.

Please understand I need to sort something out and I need solitude for that, but I love you! Please forgive me for leaving like this. I'll be back and then I will explain everything.

Love!

Mom"

25

In the meantime, Nell was sipping her water on a British Airways flight to London. She flipped from one video channel to another, unable to relax. She'd called a friend in London and asked to meet her at Heathrow tomorrow morning. Jenny was an old friend, and they hadn't seen each other for years. Nell intended to catch up with her while she figured out her next move. And since Jenny wasn't part of her regular social circle, Nell thought she would not be on the radar for some time, if David was trying to follow her route.

Jenny met her at the airport, boisterous as always. She offered her home and hospitality without the slightest hesitation. They went to her apartment in Willesden Green and spent the whole afternoon talking. Jenny was still single, still looking for the real one. They had met in Milan years ago at a fashion show. She was a fashion reporter and traveled a lot for her job. It suited her well, and because they liked similar places and had similar tastes outside fashion, she and Nell had become friends. When they had a chance, they spent time together, but did not correspond regularly.

They were also similar in appearance and age, so Jenny fit into Nell's plan well. She asked Jenny if she could borrow her passport and travel under her name. It was a little risky, but Jenny didn't mind. She reassured Nell that it wouldn't be a problem, since she was staying put in London to finish some work. Nell promised to send the passport back to her in a week; she planned to put it in a box with some used books and send it via regular mail.

After their talk, Nell crashed and fell asleep. The next morning, Jenny drove Nell to Dover, bought a ticket for the hovercraft for her, gave Nell her own passport, and gave her a big hug before departing. Nell checked her hair and makeup one more time, and put on a pair of dark glasses. The passport inspection was really only a formality; they just checked the passport to see if it was real or fake, so she passed through without any problem. She was prepared to tell the officer that she'd aged since the photo was taken, but there was no need. The security checkup was more rigorous. She was worried someone might find her own, genuine U.S. passport in her suitcase's zippered side pocket, which would be really bad for both her and Jenny. It was between two notebooks, and Nell thought wouldn't be suspicious enough for any official to check the pocket. And she was right. It went without a hitch. She was on her way to France without a trace.

She boarded the train in Calais and woke up in Paris the next day. From the Gare du Nord she called another old friend of hers, Mme Maxinne, and soon was on her way to meet her. They knew each professionally, and once Nell had given Maxinne a loan to start up her own business. Maxinne had a milliner's shop and enjoyed great sales in France and in England, but not much in the U.S., since it was uncommon to wear hats in the States. Her business was going well. She'd paid Nell back earlier than the agreed-upon time, and was very grateful for Nell's help. Because Maxinne had no connection to her U.S. shops, Nell thought she wouldn't be considered as a lead if someone was looking for her in France.

Maxinne seemed very pleased to see her, and told Nell that, even though she looked depressed and sad, she still was one sexy lady. She led Nell to a little second-floor apartment where she could stay. It was sunny, and even though it looked into the closed courtyard, it was pleasant and cheerful. The courtyard was full of plants, including a thriving fig tree. The house must have been a hundred years old but had been renovated recently, so Nell had all the creature comforts she needed. The best feature was a little room with a roof window that had been converted to an artist's studio. In the closet there were easels and painting supplies. There was also a corner office with a desk, office supplies, a computer, and a printer. There was a king-sized bed and a commode in the bedroom, a small kitchen, and a cheerful bathroom with a high window that let some natural light in. The apartment even had a little living room with two chairs, a sofa, and a flat TV on the wall. Nell was very grateful, and thanked Maxinne again and again. She promised to pay Maxinne rent and any other costs when she moved out, but Maxinne did not want to hear of it. "No, you do not owe me anything for this, my dear. You helped me when I needed it most, and because of it I can keep this little apartment for my son, who is in India right now and won't be back for another year. It just works out for both of us very well. I'll want to come and visit you, you know. I want to know the details of why you are in hiding, but I know this is not the time. Later, when you feel a little calmer about it, you can tell me."

Nell nodded gratefully; she appreciated Maxinne's discretion. She needed some time to figure out herself if she was doing the right thing or not.

"In the meantime," Maxinne continued, "I will help you with everything you need. You will need groceries and other toiletries, since my son was here a long time ago. I want you to just relax for a little while. Oh, and here's the number of a spa you should go to. Lastly, I want you to have this." She handed Nell an envelope full of cash and a list of stores and contacts if she needed anything, from a dry cleaner to a grocery store. "Use it as you need, and never hesitate to call me for anything!"

After Maxinne left, Nell looked around again, unpacked her suitcase, and sent a text to Kathy from her store-bought phone saying that she was safe. She looked at the envelope and the cash, and after going down to buy some bread and cheese, she realized Maxinne must have given her enough to live for at least a few months in Paris. She decided that, despite Maxinne's objections, she was going to pay her back at the end of her self-imposed exile.

The apartment was in the middle of the artists' district and was close to the Sacré-Coeur. Nell stopped at a used bookstore and bought a few dusty books and leaflets. At the apartment, she used the box she'd asked the store to pack them in, and put Jenny's passport into the middle of one of the books, first covering it with newspaper. She filled the rest of the space with used newspaper that were also from the bookstore. She taped it up, wrote Jenny's address on it, and wrote on the side of the box that it contained "printed matter." It helped that she'd spent a few months in France immediately after college; she could speak and use the language rudimentarily, even if no one mistook her for a Frenchwoman. On her way back to her place, she spotted a little post office, where she sent the package to Jenny in London. For the return address, she used a real Paris address that was close to her apartment, but wrote a made-up name, and hoped for her luck to hold. It did. She called Jenny and told her the books they'd talked about were on their way. Jenny was very happy that everything had worked out smoothly.

In the meantime, David and Franco were intent on finding Nell, and Chelsea helped them by providing a list of Nell's stores in Europe and the people who ran them. Franco had a contact who was good at finding airlines' computer records, and he found out that a Mrs. Preston had taken a BA flight to London, but from there he couldn't find anything under Nell's name. Since Franco also knew someone at Interpol, he could find out if she'd crossed the border, but her passport or name hadn't surfaced anywhere. So they started to search in England, particularly in London. So far there were no leads, but Kathy called them two days later to say she'd gotten a text from Nell, and that she was safe. They knew she didn't have her own cell phone with her, so it wasn't very helpful, but made them happy anyway just to hear she was all right.

26

Nell was fine during the day. But when the evening came, she found herself sitting down and looking into space, ignoring the old French romance movie on TV. After some time, she turned it off, because the images of the couple looking at each other with adoration made her sick. She was completely desperate, desolate, and empty. How could all this have happened? It was all bliss one moment and darkness in the following one. She felt a tear sliding down her cheek, but wiped it away angrily and put all her effort into just staying calm and keeping her composure. It was not easy, though. She still felt she'd made the right decision, but it would be the hardest part of her life for some time, she knew.

David was on her mind constantly. The way he smiled; the way his white teeth showed; the little crinkles around his eyes when he was happy; the way he walked; his voice; and how his eyes shined when he looked at her. It was more than missing him; she felt like she'd been torn from the inside and disassembled into small pieces. There was no life without him. But it had to be endured. She wasn't going to take away the chance to have children from the man of her dreams. He was the perfect man; he needed to have children, no question about it. Since she couldn't give them to him, she needed to let him go, no matter how hard it was. She ate some bread and cheese and tried to read a magazine, but could not. She took a long bath and tried to sleep, but was up half the night. She hoped tomorrow would be a little less depressing. *Good luck with that*, she thought.

The next day she woke up to sunshine filtering through the lace curtains, and, despite all her problems, she felt a tiny bit better.

After showering she put on a summer dress and took a stroll to see the areas around her place. It was adorable, very European and friendly. There were painters everywhere, street musicians performing, and lots of people just milling around, sitting at the cafes and having a good time. She found a small art-supply store and a delightful craft store, a well-supplied grocery, and a bakery that smelled heavenly. She also noticed that the spa Mme Maxinne had recommended was only two blocks away, and it seemed like a nice place from the outside. When she got home she called the number and made an appointment for a massage the next day.

Later that day, Nell got a text from Kathy saying that David was searching for her and committed to finding her, and that everyone missed her. When Nell got the text, it made her cry for hours, but her resolve to stay in hiding didn't falter. She was sure she needed to give David his freedom back. The pain was searing, sometimes unbearable, and she still felt her heart was in a million pieces. She considered herself a survivor and a very strong woman, so she concluded it would get better sooner or later, and until that point she just had to endure it.

The next day, Nell woke up and put on a pair of shorts and a flowery top with sandals and started to explore again just to kill time. She went to the bakery and ate a delicious croissant, then bought a baguette for dinner. Then she walked to the spa and stepped into the cool anteroom, which was decorated with black and white tiles and giant palm trees in glazed containers. It was so soothing that she almost felt better. A smiling Indian girl came out dressed in a sari. She introduced herself as Surita and took Nell's reservation. Nell complimented her on her outfit, and Surita's smile became even wider. She ushered Nell into one of the massage rooms. It was painted a very cool, pleasing peach, and several potted plants surrounded the massage table, sofa, and end table. *Whoever owns this spa must love plants and know how to grow them well, too,* Nell thought.

She sat on the sofa and sampled some refreshments while she waited for her massage therapist to show up. On the end table there were grapes and bananas, almonds and tea, club soda, and bottled water. There was even a little plate with chocolates. She took one, and discovered it was a truffle, and very good.

She was opening the club soda when the knock came. Before she could say anything, the door opened and a giant of a man appeared in the doorway. He must have been about six three, and had a body out of an anatomy book. Every muscle showed up separately with maximum definition, but without the exaggerated proportions of a body builder.

"Hi, I'm Omar. I'm very pleased to meet you. Mme Maxinne said you would be coming and asked that we treat you well, so we will, I promise." He took Nell's extended hand, and she looked as her whole palm disappeared in his hands, which were so much larger than hers. His face showed his origins were North African, probably Berber. His skin was smooth and coffee colored, and his eyes were almost completely black. His smile was very warm and disarming, which made it easy for her to feel a little more relaxed despite his tremendous size and the force she imagined he would use as a masseur. Not only that, but he was so handsome and moved with such sexuality that she felt embarrassed in an instant. His gaze was not insolent or in any way threatening, but she felt he had a built-in sex appeal, which he did not deliberately use, but simply exuded. She was terrified to think he would be touching her and handling her naked body in a few minutes, but was embarrassed to even think about it.

She was surprised by her own reaction to this stranger, but could not help it. So with as much dignity as she could muster, she said, "I'm also very pleased to meet you. If Mme Maxinne recommended you to me, you must be very good. Look, I don't want to sound like a coward, but your hands are so large, I wonder if someone else might want to start on my muscles. I haven't had a massage for years, and I just wouldn't want to be very sore. I hope you don't mind."

He laughed, showing very white, even teeth that evoked even stronger sexual feelings in Nell. She was shocked to feel such nervousness and arousal at the same time just looking at a complete stranger. She tried to look at the palm tree instead of Omar.

"I know, everyone feels I'm so large at first, but you'll see I am very gentle when I give a massage. I promise you will not get sore, but you will enjoy it. My hands will treat you well, Nell."

"Well, I don't know. I'm a little nervous, my last massage was years ago."

"Just relax and try to clear your mind of everything. You'll see, it will be a soothing experience." He came to the chair, handed her a clean folded sheet, and smiled, which transformed his face into something really appealing. She accepted the sheet without being able to even speak.

"Just put this on, and I'll be back in a few minutes. After the massage you can go to the other room to have some mud packing if you like. Surita will help you unwind there. It will be good, you'll see. And there won't be any charge for the treatments. We will do it for free, since you are a friend of Maxinne's."

He left, and Nell considered just leaving, but it would have been rude both to Omar and Mme Maxinne. She thought Omar's hands on her skin would make her anything but relaxed. On the other hand, the massage might be successful in another area: for the first time since she'd arrived in Paris, she wasn't thinking of anything she'd left behind— not her great sadness, nor David, nor Chelsea. She was, for a moment, in the present instead of staying in the past and feeling her heart bleeding. So she forced herself to be calm, put her clothes on the provided chair, and lay down on the table. It was cold, but comfortable. She still felt very weird, as if the whole experience was happening to someone else, not her. She pulled the sheets up to her chin and waited for him to return apprehensively.

The knock came, and he entered again, carrying some lotions with him. Nell noticed for the first time that he was wearing warm-up pants and an old T-shirt with torn-off sleeves. She still couldn't shake her sexual awareness of Omar's presence. *He's one sexy masseur,* she thought and tried to look anywhere else than his body or face.

He put some lotion on his huge hands and started to smooth it onto her shoulders, then onto her arms. She closed her eyes, because she did not want Omar to see what she was thinking about.

"It will be all right, chérie, you'll see. All problems go away sooner or later, time heals everything, and I will try to help you forget whatever makes you so sad. Just relax and enjoy the feelings. It'll be fine, I promise."

His hands were really gentle. Despite all that pent-up unhappiness, nervousness, and sexual awareness, she started to feel soothed and drowsy. Her muscles were rigid and bunched up from the tension that had been building in her for some time, but Omar's hands took it away and left her feeling pampered and light. By the time he pulled down her sheet to give her a massage on her trunk muscles, she did not fear it. It was a welcome relief. She was half asleep when he said, "Just rest for a while, ma chérie," and left the room.

Later, she had the mud packing, and as she finished up, she felt completely renewed and much better than before. After she'd put her clothes back on, Omar came in and said, "Please come back every day for a while. We want you to unwind and feel more relaxed. And also tell Maxinne that we are grateful she sent you here." Surita gave her some creams to use on her skin for the night and asked her to come back tomorrow midmorning. Nell agreed, went home, and was even able to read a little bit. She went for a walk and bought paint supplies and groceries for dinner. Despite her misgivings, the massage and spa seemed have given her some much-needed calm. That night was the first she slept more than six hours.

27

Chelsea spent several days searching her mother's database of European contacts, compiling a list of all the people Nell had exchanged e-mails with over the last few years. She found two more names in England she hadn't noticed before, both from the last year. She called David and gave him the names and e-mail addresses of the women. One was named Jenny, and looking at the e-mail, Chelsea thought she lived in London. *Maybe this is a lead*, she thought.

In the meantime, David had concluded that Nell's crisis must have had something to do with her visit to the gynecologist's office. She'd gone there just before she left. He needed to find out what had made her go away. She'd said in her note that she was healthy, but in light of her fleeing, he was fearful it might not be so. What else could have separated them? She was in love with him, he was sure, and she'd been eagerly looking forward to the wedding. He was miserable that she was gone. All the pent-up frustration made him work even harder to find her. Whatever her reasons, they couldn't justify a separation, he was sure of that.

Finding out medical information from a doctor wouldn't be easy, he knew. It was an advantage that he knew the doctor in question socially. He seemed like a very nice, decent guy. They'd attended some parties together, and David remembered his wife was a vivacious blond and their daughter a typical California teenager. So he placed a call to the doctor's office and asked for an appointment. The secretary said he could see the doctor for about a half hour the next morning. He then called Franco with Chelsea's new leads.

The next morning, he showed up at the doctor's waiting room and was ushered into his office. The doctor's success was visible; his office was opulent. In a few minutes he came in and greeted David with a friendly handshake. "Hi, David, looking good as usual. How can I help you? I assume you didn't come to have a physical with me." He laughed at his own joke, and David couldn't help smiling himself.

"No, Roger, I sure didn't come for a physical. I came for your help in something important. I do apologize for my request in advance, I realize it's not something you face every day, but hopefully after hearing the circumstances, you might be able to help me."

Roger sat down in a chair on David's side of the desk and gave a friendly nod. "You're making me curious. So out with it. I'll help if I can."

"Not to make a long story of it, it's about my fiancée, Nell Preston. She was here at your office a few days ago, and then she disappeared that same day. Disappeared, as in left without a word to me or her family, without even a phone call to her daughter. She left a note saying she needed to go away for at least six months, that she wasn't sick or dying, but she wanted to give me back my freedom despite still loving me. No one knows where she is, and we still haven't found her.

"I wanted to see if you can at least give me a hint about why she ran away. I know you can't disclose any information about her health or what you discussed with her, so I realize this request is pretty unusual, but I was hoping for at least a hint. Or tell me if Chelsea, her daughter, might be able to find out more, since she is her closest relative. Please, help me."

The doctor leaned back and sighed. "This isn't an easy task you're giving me! I can't tell you what we discussed, but if you think back, you can probably remember why she came back to me that day. Also, Nell is a very honest woman, so if she said in the note she was healthy, I would believe her. So do you know why she came in to see me?"

"I think it was some lab results. But what does her cholesterol or blood count have to do with our marriage? I don't get it."

"You're right, it was lab results that we discussed, and I gave her good news and bad news. Now, think about why she would come to me in the first place, and you'll figure it out yourself. You don't go to a gynecologist to find out about your cholesterol."

"You mean to find out about...fertility? Oh my God, that has to be it! She can't have a baby...right? Oh, forget I said that. Just answer one thing, Doctor. Can a lab result turn up something a physical exam wouldn't show about fertility?"

"Unfortunately, yes, my friend. That's all I can tell you, you understand. I'm sorry to hear she left. You two seem like an ideal couple, and I truly hope it works out! Best of luck!"

He shook David's hand and left the room. Without breaking his confidentiality, he'd given David the clue he was looking for. *That must be it*, he thought. Now he was sure he had the answer, he was even more determined to go after Nell as soon as he could.

How could Nell think he needed children more than he needed *her*? As much as he would have enjoyed children, he was completely happy to live with her and forget about kids. He loved her with a passion that couldn't be broken by a circumstance like this.

Wasting no time, he called Chelsea and told her they needed to talk later. Then he called Franco to see if he had any results. David was anxious beyond belief. *I'm going to find you, Nell, and we will be so happy. I can't wait, my love. Why did you leave me? We belong together, no matter what. Don't worry, I'm coming and bringing you back soon!*

28

Nell was finishing up her morning coffee and planned to chat with Mme Maxinne after that. She was beginning to feel that she could now talk about her problems and her pain. In fact, she'd even opened up about some of her circumstances to Omar during their massage sessions in the last few days. He was a very good listener and a good judge of people—or maybe only of her, Nell wasn't sure.

She hadn't meant to talk at all, but on the second day, he'd asked her who the man was that she missed so much, and why she had run away. She'd almost fallen off the table when he asked her. "How do you know that's the case, and I'm not only on vacation here?" she managed to respond.

"People on vacation are usually not depressed. I see the sadness in your eyes, chérie. I lost my own love, and I recognize the pain in others."

"Wow, are you sure you aren't a therapist in disguise? I'll tell you, if you tell me about your lost love."

Omar laughed, his white teeth showing again. "Okay, ma chérie, I'll tell you. Once upon a time, I had a beautiful fiancée who had the merriest laugh, the blondest hair, and the bluest eyes in Paris. She was soon going to make me a very happy man indeed. Then one day she crossed the road and a drunk driver hit her. She was gone in a second."

"Oh, how sad! What was her name?" asked Nell .

"Her name was Colette, and I loved her with all my heart." He was silent for a while. "Now it's your turn, Nell."

"Well, it's hard to talk about it, but as you can tell I'm in love and I'm very sad, because I can't ever have him. I can't give him a child. He's a young man, and if he marries me, he won't be able to have kids. I can't do that to him. Even if he said it was okay, eventually, his feelings would change. He'd want to have that part of his life filled, and I don't want him to resent me for being unable to give it to him.

"So I had to run when I found out. If I'd stayed to tell him about it, I couldn't have left him. I'm too much in love. I would have folded. So I ran away, just like you said. I don't think they'll be able to find me."

"Ma chérie, if he loves you as much as you love him, he *will* find you. What is going to happen is that he will come and find you and convince you to marry him. If you were my woman, that's what I'd do."

"That's very nice of you to say so."

"It's true. You can't give up on a love like that. Look at me; I still haven't recovered from losing my fiancée, and that was eight years ago. I know she's gone, and I do have an occasional lady friend, but no one has come to claim her place."

"But Omar, I don't want him to find me. He needs someone else, I'm telling you."

"No, lovely. For him, you are worth any sacrifice. Just look at you! You remind me of my fiancée. She had a smile like yours, all-encompassing and radiating happiness. She lit up the room, like you. You need to be happy again, to show it more often. Whatever you think, your man is very lucky to love you!"

"Thanks, Omar," said Nell. "You make me feel a little better. It's a waste that you don't have a new love. You're a very nice and very perceptive man."

"And a foolish one, too. Because I know you can't be mine, but I want you anyway, even if only for a while." With that he pulled her up into his arms and kissed her. It was not only completely unexpected, but surprisingly so pleasurable that she just couldn't push him away. Her last thought before letting go of all control was that she would never see David again. So why not let this gentle, sexy man give her some much-needed stress relief?

Omar picked her up like a little feather and laid her down on the sofa, where he proceeded to kiss every part of her body. Before, he'd put lotion on every inch of her; now, he licked her and nibbled her everywhere before covering her with his hard body. He was a dream lover. Nell was living in a fantasy, and let herself float away with the sensations this giant of a man evoked in her. He was gentle and slow, but persistent, and knew how to make love to every inch of her. With his patient technique, he made her want and anticipate so much that she almost screamed for release, and when finally she got it, it was like jumping from the highest mountain, complete with the sensation of weightlessness and white nirvana afterward. She was sure she wouldn't be able to move for hours. Her blissful state covered her like a blanket and sheltered her from her recent pain.

"Sorry, ma chérie, I couldn't help myself," Omar said afterward. "You're the most adorable woman. I hope you'll let me be your friend and won't hate me for loving you."

"Why would I hate you, Omar? You're very nice and very sexy, and I already felt like we were friends. I couldn't have imagined myself with any other man except David, so I'm a little surprised I let this happen. I don't regret it, though. You're a fantastic lover, and for a little while I didn't feel the pain I've had for so long. I just hope you don't feel I used you for pain relief."

"Ma chérie, you can use me for anything if it involves sex with you. I realize it will be only temporary. You will go back to your love soon, but let me pamper you in the meantime."

Nell didn't agree with that assessment, but she kept it to herself. From that moment on, she not only had massages to keep her muscles from knotting, but the best sex therapy on the planet. She hoped Omar would help her get through the present loneliness, so she could face a future on her own.

Omar took her to his apartment in the afternoons, and they watched movies together. She used the painting supplies she'd bought to make sketches of him nude, and he played with her body to keep the sadness away.

They also had long conversations about their youth. Omar had grown up in Morocco, come to France for high school, and moved to Paris to study massage therapy. When he graduated, he stayed and got a good job at the spa he worked at now. He became the favorite therapist of the old man who owned the business. The owner was an American who'd come to live in Paris twenty years ago, which was why Omar's English was so perfect. When the owner had died two years ago, he'd left the spa to Omar, so now he was the owner of a business. With all these events, Omar had almost gotten over Colette, but not completely. He knew she was gone and understood it, but still carried around a strong feeling of loss.

In turn, Nell opened up as well. Talking to him about anything just felt right and easy. She told him about Chelsea, Sam, Jack, and the plane accident, so he learned a great deal about her life. They became friends, and somehow the knowledge that their relationship was temporary didn't make it less real. She made a connection to this man, and because of his skill in distracting her and bringing out a smile, she started to be alive again, or at least feel like a normal human being.

Gradually, she also opened up about her story with David. Omar insisted that she shouldn't have run away, and forced her to examine the situation from different angles. It was strange; at first, she completely resisted his advice, but as they discussed it, she gradually began to see that there could have been better solutions. Omar said she should have talked to David and asked his opinion before making a decision. Above all, he seemed confident that Nell could make David happy even without children. It was a confidence that she lacked, but which she gradually dared to embrace. Perhaps Omar was so convincing precisely because he was a man. From a woman's mouth, it might not have been as believable, but when Omar assured her David would be okay about her infertility, she came to believe him.

She also talked to Maxinne about her problems. She soon learned that Omar and Maxinne were quite close friends. Maxinne had been the lady love of the previous spa owner, and when he'd died, she'd become something of an aunt to Omar. She'd helped him in business matters, and he helped her in the milliner's shop with rearranging the stockrooms.

Like Omar, Maxinne seemed to think that Nell had make a mistake about David. It was certainly convincing to have two people who knew her circumstances tell her that she still had a chance for happiness; that her infertility wasn't an automatic deal breaker. As Maxinne put it, they loved each other, so perhaps David would only see the infertility as a side issue, not a main issue. Maxinne was sure that not every man needed to have children to be happy; some were happy not to.

Both Omar and Maxinne seemed to be collected and intelligent people, and Nell began to trust their judgment. Perhaps they saw her situation more clearly than she did, since they were on the outside of the problem. Maybe she was making a rush decision, and maybe David and she still had a chance.

After several weeks of such discussions, Nell finally agreed that maybe she'd been wrong. When the realization came, she decided to end the affair with Omar. If there was a chance—even a tiny chance—of getting her perfect man back, then she'd stop at nothing to reclaim him.

29

Now it came down to what David wanted. Nell suspected that he had probably started an international search for her. Perhaps it was time for him to find her. So she called Jenny and asked her to disclose Maxinne's name if David or his friends called. She also asked Maxinne for a favor or two in relationship to David's search, to which Maxinne agreed. If David was serious in finding her, he'd be successful.

She sent a text to Kathy, telling her that she was okay and giving her best to Chelsea, but didn't say anything else. She hoped Chelsea would forgive her for her long absence. Then she went back to Omar and broke the news to him that it was over.

"I'm happy for you," said Omar. "You're making the right choice, and he'll be very happy to find you, ma chérie. I'm also a little sad, since I won't have you for myself anymore. I wish we could have a little more time together."

"Omar, you're very sweet. Thank you for being so understanding and for all your help. You're a great friend and a very good lover as well. I hope we can be friends in the future, but if we do see each other, we can't ever tell anyone about our fling. I mean, that would break my marriage on the spot—if I ever get there. But you can be assured that I'll always remember you, Big Berber."

"Hey, don't say good-bye yet, lovely," said Omar. He invited her back to his apartment and, instead of healing sex, they talked all afternoon. Nell gave him the nude sketches she'd made of him to keep or to throw away, whichever he chose. Since they weren't signed, they could have been by anyone. Omar said he would keep them, and if anyone ever asked, he'd say that Colette had made them. She also gave him a photography book about California. In return, he gave her a slender silver bracelet of North African design. It was beautiful, and she thought it was probably Berber or Tuareg in origin.

Omar confessed to her that their little affair made him a little more open to looking for another lady in his life. Although no one could ever replace Colette, perhaps eight years was enough time to mourn. Nell couldn't have agreed more. In fact, as she thought of Colette's blond hair and blue eyes, a germ of an idea began unfolding in her mind. She put it away for further reflection.

That evening, she ate a delicious Moroccan meal with Omar, and they watched old movies again. She felt her spirit lifting by the minute.

Over the next few days, she waited eagerly for a call from Jenny. But a week went by, and there was no news of David. Nell began to lose her nerve. Had David given up looking for her? She started to feel depressed again.

Jenny had just gotten home from work, and was about to open her apartment door, when a man came up the stairs and called to her. He introduced himself as Mr. Moss. He said he was a private investigator and that he was looking for some information about a Mrs. Preston. *So, this guy is looking for Nell,* Jenny thought. She made sure of his credentials and asked him who was in the search party, and from his answers, she felt confident that he'd been sent by David and his American detective. As Nell had instructed her to, she gave him Maxinne's name and said Nell had probably gone to France, but she didn't know for sure. Both pieces of information were just uncertain guesswork on her part, she added, because Nell hadn't shared her final destination or her plans with her.

As soon as the man had left, she called Nell and told her about the visit. It was show time. Jenny crossed her fingers for her friend, because she thought Nell would be happy with David. Nell promised to let her know about any developments.

When Nell got the news, she reacted with both excitement and fear. She called Maxinne, then went to the spa to say good-bye to Surita and visit with Omar. It was time to say good-bye to him as well. Easier said than done. He was smiling at her, but she could see the sadness. She felt sad too. She hoped she'd see him again as a friend, but it wasn't a sure bet. They went to the bakery, bought some crusty bread and cheese, and ate it in his apartment. They knew this was their farewell.

"Hey, chérie, you know I'll miss you. If I had half a chance of taking you away from your knight in shining armor, I would, but I realize it's not possible. I want you to know that if it doesn't work out for you, I'd be happy to be there for you. Even if you don't want me as your boyfriend, you can always come back and be my friend—although I would try to convince you otherwise. I do care for you, ma chérie."

"I care for you too. If I didn't have this love for David in my heart, I'd choose you in a second. The time I spent with you was joyful and carefree, despite all my desperation and sadness. I'm positive that you'll make a woman very happy if you finally let yourself commit to the present instead of the past. Look at me, I'm telling you to step out of your past, when I was clinging to mine. I'm sorry, I really am."

She hugged him, and they ate some food and talked a little more. "Tell me, Omar," she asked, "why did being with me make you think about finding someone for real? What makes me different from your other lady friends since Collette? I'm not even your type, I think."

He smiled and showed his white teeth again. *God, he's gorgeous*, she thought.

"You're different, but in a good way," he answered. "You're open and friendly, and you don't have any inhibitions. I like that. You gave yourself to me without restraint, and I felt you cared for me, not only for yourself. That's not very common.

"If we want to think about types, I usually had blond girlfriends, but often they weren't very smart. You're different; I can talk to you and have a good time even when we're not having sex. But I wanted you mostly for two things. One is your smile. When you smile, I feel happy and it warms me to my core. The second is that you've blown me away—literally. That was amazing."

"You're telling me that you never sixty-nined with someone before me? I can't believe it, I thought the French were very inventive when it came to sex!"

"Looks like I couldn't find the inventive ones, because you were the only one to do that," he laughed.

"I can't help but feel guilty about using you, though, Omar," Nell added.

"Don't. I knew you loved him when I first kissed you, and I knew you were thinking about him always. You couldn't help yourself. But it's fine, because you cared for me too. You wanted to give me pleasure, just like I wanted to give it to you." With that he kissed her as a way of saying good-bye. Then she put on her shoes and gave him one last kiss before leaving.

"I won't ever forget you, Omar. I do hope you have a happy life, and if it's possible I hope we can be friends in the future. You're one hell of a man, and any woman who wins you will be lucky beyond belief. Au revoir, mon ami."

She went home and started to organize her things for her return home. She hoped fervently that Omar was right, and that David would be willing to forgo children—and hence his own slice of immortality—for her sake. It was certainly a lot to ask of anyone. She felt anticipation building in her, and had visions of her perfect man walking through her door and back into her life again.

She felt guilty about her short affair with Omar, but she rationalized it by telling herself that she wouldn't have entered into the affair if she'd thought she had a chance of seeing David again. And after all, without Omar, she wouldn't have changed her mind about her self-imposed exile. She'd needed those long talks with him about her problems. And if he hadn't been her lover, she wouldn't have listened to him or anyone else who had a different view on the matter.

She knew it was her masculine brain again, finding excuses, but she was sure the result made it a positive thing. So all in all, she thought it was the right thing to do, and she decided not to regret it. She would always remember Omar as a very good friend who helped her heal and get back on track with her life.

30

In the meantime, Franco had informed David about the new developments. David decided to buy his ticket to France as soon as they finished talking. Paris was one destination they hadn't really considered, but now they were almost sure it was where Nell had run away to. Franco's contact was going to talk to Maxinne. Hopefully, they'd find out Nell's exact address in a matter of hours.

David shared the good news with Chelsea, and they called Franco to thank him for finding Nell. Franco promised to call with any further information, but David was too impatient to wait for the final details. He went home, started to pack, and bought a ticket to France. He'd be on his way tomorrow.

Nell made sure all the art supplies were organized and the little apartment would be left clean when she departed. Hopefully it would be soon! Maxinne had called her and told her she'd been in contact with Franco, and she estimated David would arrive in Paris in a day or two.

Nell was so excited that she was unable to read, watch TV, or even sketch anything. She made herself busy by walking through the neighborhood, taking stock and imprinting on her memory the delightful little streets and alleys close to her hideaway. She decided that she would come back, hopefully with David. They would explore this part of Paris together sometime.

She sat down at a cafe and ordered a lemonade and a pastry, watching the passersby and the birds collecting the leftovers from the boulangerie across the street. It would have been very relaxing if she hadn't been dying to see David. She wished her perfect man would come and rescue her *now*.

She mused about all the happenings of the last months, and was hit by a feeling of unreality. So many different things had happened. Life was full of surprises, for sure. Who would have thought that her stable family would be broken, that her best friend would become her best lover and the love of her life? That she would run away, only to realize she didn't want to? Now she had come full circle. She needed stability and time with David, the man of her dreams and fantasies.

She purchased a beautiful, antique flower pin at a little shop for Maxinne. This time she used her own credit card, not afraid of the trace. At the apartment she left a thank-you note and a velvet box containing the pin on a little table in the foyer. She was sure Maxinne would enjoy wearing it, and it would remind her of their short time together. When she got back at the States she planned to send something nice to Jenny as well. Without her help, she wouldn't be here.

Despite all the desperation and sadness, Nell thought this interlude had been necessary to put things into perspective. She was a firm believer in fate; she thought everything had a reason, and she just needed to find the positive meaning in it. Well, she was waiting for the positive part now, and it wasn't easy.

From the air, Paris looked like a jewel box. As David recognized its unmistakable landmarks, he felt so relieved to be so close to his woman that he couldn't stop smiling. The stewardess told everyone to prepare for their landing in Orly, buckle their seat belts, and stay put.

Despite the long flight and jet lag, he was wide-awake and excited. He closed his eyes and imagined Nell with a smile on her face, looking into his eyes. She was a woman to keep, no matter what. He wasn't sure how, but he knew he'd convince her that they belonged together, and that was that. No matter what it cost, no matter how, he needed to convince her. He was so close now; only the airport to navigate, then the border inspection, and he could go directly to the address he'd gotten from Franco.

The rest was all blurry. The landing, the passport check, the luggage pickup, and the taxi. It all melted into a slightly unfocused time, until everything became sharp again on a little street somewhere close to the Sacré-Coeur. He could see the top of the basilica from where he was, and noticed the old trees lining the streets, the cafes further down, and the people moving around in a way so typical of European cities.

He stopped in front of the appropriate apartment building. It was very old. The gate was closed, and, stepping into the entrance, he could see an enclosed, treed courtyard. The staircase led to a circular inner balcony, and he could see the numbers on the doors. He needed to find 1A, so it had to be closest to the stairs. He rang the bell and listened to the noises of the house. It was remarkably quiet, except for birds chirping in the large fig tree in the courtyard and a muted chanson coming from a few doors down.

And then the door opened, and Nell appeared. She looked the same and different all at once. She had the same beauty, but somehow looked more mature, more determined, and a little sad. Without a word she pulled him into her embrace. He stepped inside, kicked the door shut, dropped the suitcase from his hand, and started kissing her as if it were their first time ever. In a sense, it was.

"I was so hoping you would come!" she gasped. "Thanks for coming! I'm so sorry I left you, David, but I thought I didn't have a choice."

"Before you stop me, I just have to say it doesn't matter if we have kids or not," David interrupted. "I want you anyway. I want you for keeps. I want to marry you. Please, Nell, make sure you never leave me again!"

"All right, big boy! I missed you and I want you to marry me if you're sure that's what you want."

"Yeah, that *is* what I want. And now please, be quiet for a while and let me love you finally."

He pulled her free of all her clothes and pulled her to the bed that was visible through the door. He kicked the bedroom door shut, not wasting time. So here they were again, tumbling around in a hurry to get to each other, to be as close as two humans can get. She heard him mumbling something, but was not sure what it was. And anyway, it was not important. The important thing was his hands on her skin, his lips on her mouth, and his hips between her thighs. He was all hers again, and she hoped with all her heart that, this time, it was for good.

Their coupling was so hot she had a fleeting thought that the sheets would get burned. Then she again forgot everything except David being part of her. They came at the same time, forcefully clutching each other as if they never wanted to let go. She felt herself being lifted and transferred to somewhere idyllic and beautiful, and hoped David felt the same way. All her other experiences with other men were pleasurable and exciting, but sex with David was exceptional and offered an extra feeling of bonding. She really felt she was home; that fate had given her this man as a way of making her whole. David gave her not only pleasure but companionship, friendship, and security; everything a woman could ever desire from a man. She wanted to stay with him for the rest of her life.

"I missed you so much, love," whispered David. "Please, promise not to ever run out on me again. Without you, life feels pretty empty. I went on with my life and functioned, but my insides were numb and I didn't feel alive until now. I love you, you know."

"Look, if I can ever explain it, I ran away because I love you, too. I thought I couldn't take away children from the man of my dreams, no matter how much it hurt me. But I was miserable! I was so desperate, and despite my intentions, I so hoped you'd come after me. And you did. You really are my knight in shining armor. You are my *perfect man!*"

"Well, I'm very flattered you think so, and I hope that means we're not finished." He started to arouse her again, this time taking his time for slower and more refined sex, making it very hard for her to think of anything at all.

"Hey, tiger, slow down! I thought you were tired after a transatlantic flight. Are you on some aphrodisiac or something?"

"Shh. I said I missed you, didn't I?" he answered, and continued his quest to remind her of everything she'd longed for.

They completely took the sheets from the bed by the time they finished reminding each other of their physical selves, but they were incredibly happy.

After resting, they went out in search of food and started to discuss how and when they would return home. David told her about his search with Franco and Chelsea. She told him her side of the story, leaving out the part about Omar, but telling him how helpful Maxinne had been in discussing her dilemma and giving her the right advice.

"You mean to tell me we only found you because you wanted to be found? Did you let Jenny and Maxinne talk to Franco's man so I could come and take you back?" asked David.

"Hey, I have some trade secrets too, big boy. Anyway, if you hadn't found me, I'd have come home on my own soon. I realized it was wrong of me not to even discuss the future with you. I'm sorry, I was so upset, I just couldn't think straight."

"You know, love, that I'd forgive you for anything. Whatever it is I feel for you, I've never felt before. I think I can't live without you, period. So, please let me be around, okay?"

"I think I let you be *in* me, not just around me, didn't I, tiger? I promise that in the future we'll discuss any changes or bad news without me running away. Now, let's plan on going home."

And that was what they did. They booked a ticket for the next day back to San Diego and called Chelsea and Kathy. They were happy to hear the good news. Chelsea said she couldn't wait to tell Nell about the work she'd done at the store and at school. Kathy told her she was missed, and would be nice to have her boss again at the helm.

Nell also called Shellie and told her they were coming home, and that she'd be needing a bridesmaid soon. They would go ahead with the wedding as planned. David also called his friends with the news, and they went to bed planning their future together. They even got a few hours of sleep, although not many. Their separation had certainly been a big turn-on for her man, Nell observed. By the morning she was sore and so out of steam because of their make-up sex, she was sure she would sleep through her flight. As it happened, they both did. It was an uneventful flight, and the happy ending was seeing Chelsea, Franco, and Kathy waiting for them at the terminal. Finally they were home and together, as it should be.

31

The wedding was, as she'd planned, in Hawaii on the terrace of the Halekulani Hotel. Shellie was the bridesmaid and Pete was David's best man. Everyone looked terrific. Chelsea and Michelle wore light yellow dresses, and the other ladies, Shellie, Tess, and Kathy, wore darker saffron dresses. The men wore black tuxedoes with light yellow shirts and looked gorgeous. Nell wore a traditional white wedding gown. It was sleek and simple. The shoulders were bare, but the arms were covered with lace. Her flowers were plumeria and anthurium, so the light yellow was spiced up with some red. Delicate ferns and ribbons hung down from the globular bouquet. It was both elegant and simple.

Nell wanted to have a low-key event, but gave a lot of thought to the details, so it would be memorable and photogenic. She looked beautiful in her gown, especially with her tanned skin and coral lip-gloss. Her hair was simple, too. She wore a plumeria close to one ear and piled her red hair a little higher on her head. All in all, she was very happy with the result.

She had danced with Pete and Ryan, Michelle's boyfriend Tim, and even Kathy's longtime companion John, and now it was almost time for her to be with her "pretty boy." (David and Pete were teasing each other mercilessly, so she'd found out his nickname.) But first, she had a suggestion to make to Shellie. Her bridesmaid looked very beautiful, but was there without a date. Nell hooked her arm through Shellie's and said, "Listen, I just wanted to tell you what a fantastic time I had in Paris. You know most of it already. It was relaxing and gave me some time just to reflect on things. Maybe you could do the same. Maxinne was telling me that her son is in India for another half a year or so, and if I need to use the apartment I'm welcome to. I think you should go for a little while. I think it would be *really* good for you."

"Okay, I'll consider it," said Shellie. "I have work on this project we started for another week, but after that I'll have a few weeks to spare. Are you sure Maxinne wouldn't mind?"

"Look, I paid for my expenses, and David put together a pretty good ad campaign for her gratis, just to repay her help. She's raking in all kinds of business because of it, and I think she's very grateful to both of us."

"But how do I enter the picture, darling?" Shellie pressed.

"Hey, you're one of my dearest friends, and you need a little relaxation. I can't think of a better place that Paris. I think that would qualify as a reason. I'm also very grateful to you for helping me organize the wedding and for being there for me every minute. So can I call her?"

"Yeah, you can call her. Especially since that jerk ex of mine just found a younger woman and told me about his impending engagement. I need to think of something other than that!"

"Attagirl! I'll call tomorrow. Maxinne will help you; she knows all the best places to relax in town. She'll be happy to see a friend of mine, I promise you that," said Nell. She had done her best; now it was up to nature, coincidence, and chemistry. If she was right, Shellie would come back from Paris a happier woman.

And now, Nell needed to give her attention back to her man, because it looked as he was about to literally push Shellie out of the way to take his place by her side. Nell was very happy to be pulled up into his embrace. They said good night to everyone and wished them a good time, then disappeared into their suite, which was quiet and inviting, alight with candles and strewn with flowers. A champagne cooler stood beside the enormous bed, next to a plate of strawberries and chocolate. She was taken with all the care and consideration these touches showed, even if they were clichés.

They did not have anything to drink or eat at first. They had each other instead. David took care removing the dress from her, so it wouldn't be torn. The ceremony and the entertaining had been hard work and tiring, but their passion was even greater, so they ended up tangled on the bed in minutes. She still could not believe her luck: this outstanding man had just vowed to be with her for keeps.

"Hey, pretty boy, how did I attract you, being so average and mundane? You're *so* sexy, I don't think there's really a good word for it."

Between kisses and caresses he answered her teasingly, "See, sweetheart, that's the problem with you. You always want to talk about things. I think we should enjoy ourselves instead. I have to add, though, that that's the only flaw I can see. No other complaints! As far as sexiness, I don't think you need to feel inferior, even to me."

"*Even* to you! You conceited, egoistical…uhh, I can't talk if you do that."

"Good!"

He took his time before his release, so she could have a few fantastic orgasms first. He really enjoyed the fact that she was like an instrument to play on; no touch or intimacy was without a delightful answer. He felt this was the first time in his life he could let his guard down completely with someone else. It made his pleasures even more pronounced and more lasting.

As he drifted off to sleep, he thought it was different with Nell, because she'd been his friend first. They were close and intimate before they'd ever made physical contact. She was already dozing off, and her hair was all messy and fanned out on his shoulder. *It's going to be nice to wake up with her on my side every morning,* he thought at last, and then he slept.

32

They came back from the honeymoon so sated and happy, it was hard to adjust to everyday life. But eventually they got back to work at their businesses, reconnected with their friends, and settled down to their new way of life. Nell and David spent half their time at the house, the other half at the condo. They even went on a trip together to Italy, visiting Milan, Venice, and Florence, where David started an ad campaign for a new customer. They had a wonderful time. In the States, everyone noticed how happy they were; even Sam remarked to Nell that, despite the circumstances, he was really happy for them.

As for Shellie, she took a few weeks to fly to Paris and had a great time. When she came back, she told Nell that she'd met an incredibly nice man who owned a spa. His name was Omar, and he was originally from Morocco. He was going to visit her in a few weeks, and Shellie said she thought they were in love. She told Nell they were looking into opening a spa in San Diego, so he could relocate and be with her.

Nell was very happy about the news and called Maxinne to thank her for introducing Omar and Shellie. It had just been a hunch on her part, but somehow she'd had a feeling Omar and Shellie would like each other immensely. Shellie was a real California girl, all smiles, blond looks, and easy-going personality. And Omar seemed finally ready to find his woman of the present.

⌇

A few months after the wedding, Nell began to feel a bit strange. She felt bloated, and her abdomen felt tender around the area she knew held her ovaries. She assumed she had a cyst, since they were pretty common at her age. She scheduled an appointment with her gynecologist, hoping he'd be willing to offer traditional hormone treatment instead of the surgical solution, a laparoscopy. She was nervous, but David comforted her, telling her not to get overly concerned before she knew all the facts.

She tried to follow his advice, but her palms were still a little damp as she walked into the doctor's office. The doctor was very happy to see her, and gave her a physical exam and some blood tests. He said he hadn't seen any cysts, but would call her if he found any problems next week when the tests came back.

As she waited the following week, she still felt out of sorts. She tried to convince herself that her fatigue and nausea were unimportant. But if it wasn't a cyst, what could it be? She was afraid it was cancer or something equally bad, since she usually was so healthy. Then she convinced herself of the opposite: it had to be something banal, like a low-grade infection. She needed answers soon, or she'd drive herself crazy.

Finally the day of her second appointment arrived, and she sat waiting in the room for her nice doctor to come in. He came in smiling so broadly, she knew right away it couldn't be cancer. He pumped her hand and told her straight away, "Nell, you're not going to believe this—I couldn't believe it—but it's true! You're pregnant! I know I said it wasn't possible, but somehow it's still the case."

"You really mean it? Really?" Nell could hardly speak.

"Yes, looks like you were so utterly lucky, you got your infinitely small chance. Congratulations!"

"Will...do I have a good chance of keeping it? I couldn't bear a miscarriage..."

"Don't worry. If we're over the hurdle of getting pregnant, I don't see any reason for you not to have a perfectly normal nine months. You're about six weeks along. Didn't you notice your missing period?"

"I had some light bleeding, so I just thought it was different because I might have a cyst. I'm so blown away!" She was so moved, a tear started down her cheek. She said she needed to call David, and the doctor gave her a hug and left her alone to call her husband with the good news.

David was as shocked as she was, and said he'd meet her at home in half an hour. He sounded like the happiest man on earth, she thought. Then the doctor came back and gave her instructions, and made a new appointment for the first ultrasound, so she and David could see their little offspring. He also told her that the symptoms she felt were all part of her pregnancy, and that she might experience mood swings and emotional changes, like crying easily. She knew that must be true, because she was still teary-eyed.

Then she went home and waited for David to arrive, so they could share the most important news of their married life. He deserved it and she deserved it, but it still was a miracle of fate. She felt very grateful to nature, and at the same time, she immediately started to worry about the pregnancy. Then David came home and gave her all the support she needed to take the worries right out of her head. He was extraordinarily positive and happy. Now they had to explore a new dimension together, parenthood. She knew it wasn't going to be easy, but they would do it together, and it would be a great experience.

Luckily, the doctor was right: her pregnancy went along without any problems. She gave birth to a healthy baby boy. Despite all the happiness involved in waiting for him, Nell was grateful to leave the swollen ankles and terrible heartburn behind her. They named the little boy Simon, and enjoyed the beginning of their parenthood. All of their friends came by and expressed their joy, praising the little baby to the sky to his happy parents.

As for Nell, she felt very positive. She looked at the little boy as a new beginning that the universe had granted her. She knew it was her habit to compare her little world with that of the universe, but could not help it. She was sure that never had a cosmic event had bigger impact on her than this one. Stardust had coalesced, again giving her a chance to capture a small part of the future. And even more importantly, David now had that chance for himself as well. That made her even happier. She just wished she could see the future now, to know how their genes would turn out in the future, where their offspring would end up, and what kind of a world they would build for themselves. *Oh well, not all wishes are granted, but that's okay*, Nell thought, and smiled at her pretty boy.

33

Four years passed. Simon entered preschool, enchanting everyone with his happy, easygoing behavior. His parents were taken with him, completely proud of his demeanor and his cute looks. Nell could tell that he was going to be a lady-killer. He was social and smart, and he had friends already. He liked preschool, and despite everybody spoiling him, stayed very even tempered and sweet. Nell thought he would be like his father. He was an only child in some ways, but still shared his toys with his playmates. His only problem was stubbornness and sometimes being too friendly with anyone. If there was anything missing from the child, it was shyness. Both David and Nell thought they'd won the lotto ending up with Simon, and all their family and friends shared their joy and their love for the little boy.

As for Shellie, she married Omar two years after their engagement. They lived in San Diego, sometimes going back to Paris for a few months, where Surita had the spa under control. The new spa in San Diego was a very modern facility and soon proved popular. Shellie expanded her business and started a little shop in Paris, and also seemed to be succeeding.

Recently, Nell had gotten a call from her: Shellie was pregnant and ecstatic. "So, sweetie," Shellie gushed, "tell me all about child rearing, since you're just ahead of me. It'll be fantastic! Maybe our kids will end up marrying each other!"

"Maybe, or maybe not. How do you know it'll be a little girl? It might be a little Omar for all you know."

"Yeah, it's too early to tell, but somehow I just know. You'll see." They talked and laughed and shared advice on pregnancy, marriage, and life. Nell felt very grateful to have friends like her.

The good news got her thinking about her older children, Sam and Chelsea. Sam was still not married, but he'd been seeing a woman for two years now, so Nell was crossing her fingers that she would be the one for him. She was a friendly, smiling girl, good to look at, too. She adored Sam and was very patient about waiting for him to solidify their relationship. Nell hoped it would work out for him. He certainly deserved a good woman at his side.

David had also told Nell recently that Julie had remarried and lived somewhere in the Midwest with her new husband. He'd run into his ex-mother-in-law, and she was very happy to inform him that she'd soon be a grandmother. Julie was expecting in the fall. It made Nell happy to know that her life with David had not left devastation behind. She wished Julie and her parents all the happiness in the world.

She was also grateful Chelsea seemed to feel no bitterness or resentment about her new family at all. In fact, she got along swimmingly with David, and she adored her little brother.

At that moment, her phone rang. It was Chelsea. *Speak of the devil*, Nell thought.

"Mom, I have to see you tonight. I have to tell you something!" Chelsea said excitedly.

"Okay! I'll see you tonight at home, all right?"

"Sure, I'll drive down!" Chelsea replied. She was going to college in San Diego, but was on an assignment up in L.A. for three weeks. She came home sometimes, or just stayed with Michelle. They were still best friends, went to the same university, and now were roommates.

Michelle was between boyfriends, and Chelsea was in a similar situation. She still went out with Ryan from time to time, but Nell felt it wasn't going much further. Ryan had gone to work for an accounting firm and wouldn't consider further education. Nell thought Chelsea would probably meet someone with more similar interests, either at university or through swimming or horseback riding. She and Michelle had already been approached by several young men at polo matches. They were beautiful, smart, athletic, and educated girls, so they had a lot to offer. Neither of them was very wealthy, but neither was poor either, so they could chose partners they really liked, Nell thought.

$\backsim$

"Hi, Mom!" Chelsea burst through the door. "Oh, you look so good! Not to mention this little fellow next to you!" She picked up Simon and kissed both his cheeks. The "little fellow" gave her a big hug and was very happy with the attention. Then they all went out to the deck and let Simon play in the sandbox, while they sat next to each other and sipped lemonade. Nell finally prompted her daughter and said, "So, tell me, what happened?"

"Mom, you won't believe this—I found the perfect man! I think I'm in love! I'm going to marry him, I swear."

"Hey, slow down! I assume it's not Ryan we're talking about?"

"Of course not! I'm so over that. Thomas is so much better in every way!"

"Do I know him? And if not, would I approve of him?"

"You've never met him, but you'll absolutely love him, Mom! He's the smartest in his class. He's a marine biologist and he has these adventures at sea, they go out to different atolls and examine the life cycles and other parameters of the corals and the fauna there. He's an Adonis, Mom. Not only is he the best-looking man

I've ever seen, but he's so sharp and dedicated, I just cannot even begin to tell you..."

"So, are you going to invite him to that party you and Michelle are talking about next week?"

"See, that's the only problem. I'm not going with him. He dates this empty-headed Fiona girl, you know, a cheerleader. God, I hate her! But it's not a problem. I'm going to have this guy for myself, Mom! I promise!"

"Oh boy!" said Nell teasingly.

"Don't worry, Mom. I'm sure as soon as I get close enough to have a real conversation with him, he'll fall for me. That Fiona has no idea about anything except soap operas. I'm smart, and I'm going to look sexy for this party, so I can't fail! I'm going to have him!"

"Well, I don't doubt you could do it, but are you sure he's the man you really want?"

"Yes, Mom! I just *know* he's the perfect man for me! He's smart and sexy and educated... he's friendly and loves science and the outdoors and the water...and he loves adventures just like me. How much better can I do?"

"So be it then, love!" Nell smiled. She knew exactly what Chelsea meant, so she was sure she could do it. She was her girl, after all. And crazy as it might sound, if they were good at anything, it was finding the perfect man.

The Author

Mitzi Penzes grew up in Hungary, where she trained and practiced as a neurologist. She has lived in the United States for the last twenty-five years, where she pursued a career in lab management. She lives with her son, husband, and cat in Napa, California.

Photo by Marissa Carlisle